MADIGAN

MADIGAN

R. Howard Trembly

To a Patriot

R. H. *[signature]*

CREATIVE ARTS BOOK COMPANY
Berkeley • California 1999

To the men and women of the West of bygone days.

And to Chris and Jeff, who live by the Western Creed of hard work, integrity, and helping their fellow man.

And to Karen, who would have made the Old West proud.

MADIGAN

CHAPTER 1

The big Irishman struck the match to the side of his pant leg with a quick upward movement of the hand and watched as it came to life in a stab of yellow-white flame. Holding the neatly wrapped bundle of six dynamite sticks in his other hand, a humorless smile spread across his sinister face as he put the flame to the fuse and watched it start to burn in a shower of sparks. Harry O'Neill's six-feet, two-inch body of pile-driving muscle shook with anticipation at the thought of what he was about to do. The day was cool, but O'Neill felt a hot flash of evil move down his spine until beads of grime-filled perspiration broke out on his forehead.

A gust of cold wind coming up the steep canyon wall from below carried a few sparks from the dynamite fuse into a clump of dry grass at O'Neill's feet, catching it on fire. But the Irishman ignored it, keeping all his attention on the man camped below while the quick-burning fuse grew shorter.

As O'Neill drew in a slow, deep breath, his cruel, hard eyes narrowed as one imagined a hawk might do just before the kill. But this darkly tanned face was no hawk's face; covered with deep scar-like lines that gave it an ominous, almost sadistic appearance under a crop of short blazing red hair that somehow looked out of place was the face of a cold-blooded butcher—a killer that in a few seconds would blow the man called Madigan to hell and back. With one powerful throw, O'Neill hurled the deadly packet in a high arc toward his unsuspecting victim below.

1

As if in slow motion, the smoking bomb sailed outward, leaving a wispy thin trail of white smoke behind it. O'Neill, unable to contain himself any longer at the imminent revenge he was about to experience, let forth with a burst of laughter that reverberated around the canyon walls like cannon fire. It was all the warning the man below needed.

In a fragment of a second, Madigan threw himself to the ground while palming his Colt in one easy motion. Like an athlete trained from years of practice, Madigan's powerfully built body sprang into action. While his vision tunneled in on the target, he cocked the hammer and squeezed the trigger of his .44. Two explosions sounded as one, and the concussion and searing heat drew the air from Madigan's lungs while pinning him to the ground like a swat from a giant fly swatter.

On the canyon rim above, O'Neill was caught completely off guard, not even having time to duck out of the way. At the burst, the shock wave rolled up the canyon wall like a fast-moving dust storm, slamming O'Neill backward off his feet and momentarily knocking him unconscious. Suddenly coming back to his senses, he was astonished at what had happened. Although he could not believe that any man was that fast and lethal with a six-gun, his own eyes told him it was true.

Picking himself off the ground, he cursed the air around him to vent what had happened while quickly wiping the dust from his face and hair. O'Neill knew at this time and place there was only one decision to be made. The killer brushed the debris off the front of his shirt, then quickly caught his horse, swung into the saddle, and rode away at a full gallop, still damning the day like a man gone mad. If Captain Madigan was still alive, there would be another day, and with it, another opportunity. But now the odds were no longer in O'Neill's favor.

It had only been a few weeks since Madigan had resigned from the army to do some prospecting and he had no way of knowing O'Neill was a free man. Now lying here dazed, one thought kept creeping through the fog into his mind: he had to stay alive and find the man whose laugh he would never forget, the demented laugh of the only man crazy enough to carry out this deed, the one and only Harry O'Neill.

The explosion was just far enough away to hurt Madigan but not quite kill him. He could feel the warm blood dripping around his eyes and ears from the concussion, and Madigan knew it was a miracle he could still see at all. Every muscle in his body ached and from time to time he coughed up bright red blood. Rolling painfully over on his back he raised up on one elbow and turned his head to look around.

There laying in the dirt some fifty feet away were the bodies of his horse and pack mule. The explosion had been much closer to the animals and it was their bodies that had absorbed the full blast, shielding Madigan from its deadly destruction. Silently he swore an oath to kill Harry O'Neill if it took the rest of his life. Then everything faded to black.

He must have laid unconscious for hours before coming to again. When he did regain consciousness it was little more than a walking daze, a fog, from which everything reeled and danced before him. Without a horse and only the water in his canteens, it was safe to say he was in a bad situation. Being extremely weak from loss of blood didn't help matters either. Even the smallest exertion made Madigan's head reel and he was unsure whether any water would stay down, but he would not give up to the pain. He would force himself to go on—to live—if for no reason other than to make O'Neill pay for this and the other crimes he had committed.

Being a man that was used to taking care of himself, Madigan crawled to his canteen and took a long slow drink of the cold water, letting it settle in his stomach before chancing to move, then taking his knife, he cut his extra shirt into strips. Within the hour he'd cleaned and bound his wounds. Madigan felt a little better afterward and to his relief was no longer coughing up blood, although his insides felt like they were on fire every time he took another sip of water. Looking toward the west, he judged by the sun that it would be dark in one, maybe two hours at the most.

One thing Madigan knew for sure was that he would have to move out of the area quickly no matter how much agony he was in. After dark his animals' remains would more than likely bring in a bear or pack of wolves. He was in no shape to tangle with either, so he carefully hid his saddle and pack where he would be able to find them later, after first hanging the extra food from the pack out of reach of any bear. A bear may not be able to see well, but it sure could smell food and unless it was hung out of reach, it would stop at nothing to get at it. Then Madigan put the rest of the jerky in his coat pocket and started off at a slow walk.

In the fog of Madigan's confused mind, he remembered hearing it said that the smell of a wounded man would draw wolves from miles away. He didn't know if it was true or not, but it wasn't a pleasant thought as he stumbled slowly through the trees. While it was still light he could drive them off with his Winchester, but come nightfall the advantage fell heavily in the wolves' favor. Madigan knew he needed to find shelter soon. Being weak and wounded, he no doubt would be the number one item on some predator's menu. Wouldn't matter if it were a wolf, bear, or mountain lion. Any one of them would have an easy time of it with the shape he was in. He had to stay alert no matter what.

Slowly, the realization came into his dazed mind that this very morning he had passed a small rawhide ranch. It wasn't much, just a rough hewn log cabin, cookshack, and bunkhouse with a few fences stuck in the middle of a small meadow. Not wanting to waste time, even though the thought of hot food was tempting, Madigan had kept to the ridge. But he had taken sharp notice of the smoke coming from the chimney of the cookshack.

Now, he reasoned, with any luck he could be back to the outfit by next morning, if the wolves didn't get him first.

Night fell and with it a crispness reminded him that spring was late this year, and there was still the possibility of snow in these higher mountain valleys. If it began snowing, Madigan's chances of survival would drop drastically.

He was pondering this possibility when somewhere off to his left an owl hooted at something passing through the night. Several times deer crossed in front of him, stopping to take a quick look before moving on, somehow sensing that he was not a threat to them.

Then he heard the cry of a wolf a short distance away, answered by another, then another. At the howl of the wolf, Madigan froze in his tracks not daring to move while listening for any noise of the wolves coming closer. He glanced around in a desperate search for a tree that would get him high enough off the ground when the wolves came. Soon there was another cry, this time more distant than the last, then another even more distant, and Madigan realized to his great relief that he was downwind from the wolves and that they were more than likely honing in on his dead animals. Had he chosen to stay instead of moving on into the night, he would have been their prey and more'n likely part of their meal by morning. He prayed none would cross his scent on its way to the carcasses of his horse and mule.

Soon a light mist began to fall. Pulling his coat tighter around his neck trying to stay warm, he switched his rifle from one hand to the other keeping the other hand in a pocket to prevent his fingers from going numb. Through the night he walked, gritting his teeth at the pain.

An hour after first light he spotted the rawhider's cabin down in the small valley. Smoke curled up from the chimney which meant it would be warm inside. And right now what he needed most was to get some warmth back in his bones. He hoped the rancher would be friendly.

"Hello, the cabin!" he yelled with all the strength he had left when a hundred yards out. For a long minute nothing happened and he wondered if he'd been heard, then a rifle barrel was suddenly thrust out between the shutters of the one lone window in the front of the cabin.

"Who be it that disturbs me home?" came a voice with a strong Scottish accent.

From the sound of it, Madigan wasn't going to be welcome. But welcome or not, he would freeze if he didn't get warm soon.

"Sam Madigan, lately of the U.S. Cavalry. I'm hurt and cold," he said in a weak voice. Another moment of silence.

"Well then, don't just stand there like a fool, Captain. Come in where it's warm and a fresh pot of coffee's brewing on the stove."

Madigan had just started toward the door when a strange sound began to drift eerily from within the cabin walls. He stopped to listen—that sound. He would recognize it anywhere. The man was obviously one of the worst players of the pipes Madigan had ever heard. The sound rose and fell, whimpered and squawked, then peaked with ear-splitting authority before falling off to a whisper, sounding like the death squeal of a mortally wounded rabbit.

Pushing the door open, he was not surprised to see Sergeant Golden Husbands sitting there huffing on the old bagpipes he'd carried with him since he was a boy fresh from the highlands of Scotland.

Looking up, the Scotsman grinned. "Thought I'd welcome you right proper, laddie," he said thrusting a big paw into Madigan's shivering hand.

"Been a long time, Sergeant. See you can't play those windbags any better than you used to," Madigan said weakly, nodding toward the patched and battered bagpipes.

"You never were one for the sweet sound of the highlands were you, laddie?" The Scot leaned over and turned up the coal oil lamp that sat beside him on a small table. "Well, look at you, laddie! Seems you been sitting too close to the fire," he said shaking his head in bewilderment. "We better get you patched up. How'd you be gettin' those nasty burns, me friend?"

While the Scotsman cleaned and bound his wounds, Madigan explained what had happened the day before and how he'd walked all night to get to the cabin. Goldie made him some bacon and eggs and afterward showed him to the cot in the corner.

"You can sleep the day through if you have a mind to. You don't have to worry about O'Neill hunting you here," the Scot said as he pulled the blanket over the wounded man. "I've got a couple of men working for me and I'll have them stay close by in case that swamp lizard tries anything.

"Best thing for you is to get as much rest as you can. I'll not play you to sleep with the pipes being you are not a true music lover and all," he said, chuckling.

"By the way," the Scotsman asked, "why is O'Neill hunting you?" Madigan's jaw tightened against the pain, then slowly relaxed.

"You wouldn't have known about it, Sergeant, 'cause you had already mustered out of the Cavalry by then. But about six or seven months ago O'Neill raped and murdered one of the enlisted men's wives, buried her body, and went about his business as if nothing had happened. Most people believed the girl had run away with a drummer on one of the wagon trains that came through the fort. You know it happened all the time, a young girl marries a soldier to get away from her folks, then finds life at the fort worse than what she ran away from. She was just about forgotten by everyone except her husband. Girls take off with drummers all the time, just a fact of life on the frontier.

"Then one night O'Neill was in town drinking with some of his friends. You know how he liked to drink. Always said he could hold it but couldn't. Anyway, he really tied one on this night. Got to bragging and it slipped out that Alice Jane—that was the dead girl's name—had let him have his way with her. Anyway, that's the way O'Neill told it."

"O'Neill never could keep his mouth shut when he had booze in his belly!" Goldie injected.

"This got back to the fort and we started a quiet investigation into the matter, but we couldn't find anything with so many trains coming through the fort headed on the Oregon Trail, so we were forced to let it drop.

"Then old Hairless Jones—you remember Jones, one of the best trappers in those parts—came in one night with Alice Jane's body wrapped in blankets. Seems O'Neill hadn't put enough dirt over her after he killed her. Jones saw a wolf pulling at a piece of cloth sticking out of the ground and investigated.

"When Jones brought the body in, O'Neill was out of the fort on patrol. Somehow he got wind of the discovery and hightailed it out of there. I was the one sent to bring him back in to stand trial and that's what I did.

"He was found guilty of murder and sentenced to be hanged the following day. Funny thing, all the time I was bringing him back to the fort he acted as if he blamed me for his troubles. Didn't matter that he killed the girl and all that. Just blamed me for catching him. Later after the trial, he said he'd see me dead before he hanged. Just the threat of a mad man, I figured. Anyway, the next day he'd hang and that would be that. Only thing was, one of his friends slipped a gun to him that night and he shot the guard and got away."

"Seems like he almost made good on that promise," Goldie said. "Now you better try to get some sleep and let your body heal."

Madigan nodded his head in agreement and laid back on the cot. Within a few minutes he was dead to the world. It was already dark when he awoke to find Goldie coming through the door carrying his saddle. The rest of his pack was laid against the wall next to the door.

"Had one of me boys ride up and pick these up while you was sleeping," he said, pointing to Madigan's things. Goldie looked at the pack and smiled. "See you still be carrying the Sharps."

"Never know when I might run across a herd of buffalo.

Did the wolves get to my horse last night?"

"A pack of them mangy critters did until a grizzly came along and ran them off. Between the wolves and the bear, they really made a feast of your animals. Made me hired man really nervous getting your things out of there. Wasn't too worried about the wolves in the daylight, but figured the bear might still be hanging around for another meal. Did take a chance and looked around up on the top of the cliff, though. From the tracks he saw, O'Neill must've hightailed it out of there the minute he threw the dynamite. Made a beeline clean out of the county, from what me man tells me."

Madigan was quiet for a long moment. "She was a good horse," he said sadly.

For two days Madigan stayed in bed, letting his strength return. On the third day he was up before first light, out chopping wood for the cook stove when Goldie slipped up to him.

"You'll be in need of another horse and I may have just the animal for you," he said cheerfully.

Motioning Madigan to follow, he led the way down a narrow path to a corral hidden in the trees. The bunkhouse stood a little to the side. They were well hidden, for Madigan had barely seen them when he rode through the area the morning of the attack.

The bunkhouse door opened as they approached and a man in his early sixties holding a rifle stepped out and waved at them, then moved back inside out of the cold.

"That's Jones," Goldie said. "He's a good man to have around in a fight. If O'Neill had come sneakin' around here, he'd have to work to keep his hide. Jones had a run-in with that coyote himself a few years back and would like nothing more than to catch him in his sights."

They approached a gate and stopped. In the corral stood the most magnificent buckskin stallion Madigan had ever seen. When the horse saw the men approach he snorted, then pawed the ground with his hoof, daring them to come closer.

"He's a mighty fine-looking animal," Madigan said, impressed with the great horse before them.

"That's what I thought too when I first laid me eyes on him. Took all three of us to corner him so I could get a rope over his neck."

Madigan saw that the horse's hind legs were hobbled and said as much. Knowing Goldie to be a gentle man, except in battle, he was puzzled as to why. The answer came shortly.

"When we first tried to catch him, we used a brush corral and chased him into it along with some of his mares," Goldie explained. "He jumped the fence like he had wings. Later that night he sneaked back and chewed through the rope that held the mares, turning them all loose and ruining two weeks' work for us. So when we finally got a rope on him we put the hobbles on—put 'em on his back legs so he wouldn't chew through them. You can bet it was a fight getting them on without getting our heads kicked in. Since then he's been pretty quiet as long as we keep our distance.

"Just no other way to keep him from taking off again. Hated to do it to such a fine animal but there was no other way," he said nodding toward the hobbles. "Anyway, he's not me problem any more," Goldie said with a laugh.

"What do you mean?"

"Why, laddie, you are his owner now! Way I see it, by giving him to you, I'll rid me-self of two problems: I won't have to train him, and he won't be 'round to stir up me mares any more."

Madigan started to protest, but Goldie stopped him with a wave of the hand.

"Captain, I've not forgotten the time I was laying in that buffalo wallow with only one bullet left and Sioux all around ready to take me scalp.

"I was just getting ready to put that bullet in me brain when you came a riding and shootin' right through them Injuns. If you remember, you brought me a horse that day and I've never forgotten."

"You thick-skinned old Indian fighter! That was your own horse I brought you!" Madigan laughed.

"If you remember, Captain, it belonged to those Sioux when you grabbed it, so I'm just returning the favor. I'll not take no for an answer," he added, rolling up his sleeves in a mock show of anger.

Well, that buckskin was a mighty fine horse and Madigan wasn't too fond of walking. And besides, it wasn't going to be a picnic getting this horse to wear a saddle, let alone keeping himself in that saddle.

"I guess you talked me into it," he said shaking his head. "I reckon now it's either me breakin' him or him breakin' me."

For the next two weeks Madigan worked with the buckskin in the evenings. During the day he'd ride out with Goldie or one of his men on one of the extra mares, cleaning out the water holes and doing whatever else needed tending.

Gradually the stallion came around to Madigan's way of thinking, but not until after Madigan was thrown a good number of times. After a while he came to realize Madigan wasn't going to give up, and he let him climb into the saddle with just a little resistance. He even seemed to like Madigan's presence around him. Before long they were riding out for miles at a time, the powerful stallion enjoying it as much as the man.

Madigan spent so much time with the horse he almost forgot about O'Neill. At any rate, he wasn't going off half-cocked for revenge anymore. Besides, Madigan knew that sooner or later O'Neill would come to him no matter where he was.

Then one cool morning it was time for him to say good-bye to Goldie and his men. By nightfall, he was twenty miles out on his way to Cooper Springs, where he camped by a little stream while the buckskin grazed nearby.

He stayed for a few days at the little town of Cooper Springs, getting new supplies and a packhorse, then decided to get on with his life. A friend once offered him a job on his ranch in California. He'd never been to California but had heard many stories of riches to be gotten there for the taking.

Madigan was willing to take his share as long as it didn't belong to anyone who came first.

The ranch down California way seemed like a blessing. He knew it would mean hard work, but he never ran from good, honest work in his life. Madigan even planned to bypass the gold fields on his way to the ranch. Course, a man on the move for weeks on end may get a little crossed up now and then, so no tellin' where he might wander through in the days ahead.

He was riding along lost in his thoughts when the buckskin shied, then perked his ears forward. The trail he was on didn't show much use. Madigan liked it that way when he was a mind to get someplace. To his right, up a small slope, was a stand of pine along with a few boulders scattered here and there.

He moved the buckskin and his packhorse into the trees and waited, for the stallion also sensed something ahead that might mean trouble. When you lived as Madigan did, you learned to take a good long look before you leaped. So he waited for whatever spooked the buckskin to either show itself or move away.

There were grizzly in this part of the country, and the last thing he wanted to do was come upon a sow with her cubs in tow. If surprised, they might charge anything that looked like a threat to them.

When a grizzly came at you, there wasn't much chance for you to outrun her. For short distances, Madigan heard tell they could outrun a horse. Maybe so, maybe not, but he wasn't in a hurry to find out.

Wasn't long before some dust showed down the trail. From the looks of it, he guessed two, maybe three riders were coming. Madigan slipped the thong off the hammer of his Colt, then checked to make sure it was loaded. It was, so he placed it back in its holster, but not as tight as it had been before. He also checked his Winchester. It never paid to get careless.

If it was trouble coming, he would be ready, at least as ready as a man could be, and Madigan didn't have long to wait. Three riders were walking their horses along the trail below him. He hadn't been seen yet, so he backed the buckskin further into the trees and waited.

"What in the heck!" Madigan said disgustedly to himself when he saw that the riders trailed two women prisoners along with them. He bit his lip hard to keep back the anger when he saw that both the women were unclothed, hands tied together in front of them, their skin burned dark from the sun.

The prisoners, both on one horse, were forced to ride between the two men in the lead, while the other man followed up behind. It was a dangerous situation and Madigan would have to act fast if he was going to do the women any good. It seemed like forever before they got within range, so all he could do was wait. And the longer Madigan waited, the more furious he got.

Madigan let out a silent curse as he pulled his rifle out of its scabbard while he nudged the buckskin into plain view of the riders below.

"Hold up down there!" he ordered as he took a bead on the hombre closest to him. The rider was an ugly beast of a man with a long scar across his forehead, a Mexican with dirty hair to match his clothes. When he turned toward Madigan he smiled with black teeth, a stub of a dead cigar protruding from between his lips. The riders stopped.

"What you want up there? We do you no harm!"

"Cut those women loose!" Madigan ordered as he levered a round into his rifle.

Scar Face turned sideways in his saddle and nudged his horse forward out of line with the women. Wiping his arm across his forehead, he grinned back at Madigan.

"You not understand! These our wives! They been unfaithful to us. We only teach them a lesson." While he talked, the second man eased up beside him, the third man staying behind.

"We mean you no harm. Why you not come down so we can talk? Maybe you want women for yourself?"

Both men laughed, and as they did the second rider casually eased his horse up behind the man with the scar. At the same instant one of the women pulled her hands to her mouth in fear. It was all the warning Madigan needed. He fired, then quickly levered another round into the chamber of his smoking Winchester .44-40. It was not needed, for the bullet hit true, knocking the scar-faced man out of his saddle and into the rider behind him. Both fell to the ground with a thud and lay still.

What the hell did he get himself into this time, Madigan wondered as he assessed the situation, still keeping the rifle to his shoulder in case he needed to fire again.

In the moment it took for the last man to realize what had happened, the two women spun their horse around and kicked it into action, running their gelding headlong into the Mexican's mount, knocking the rider off balance. As he fell to the ground in a heap, the two women were on him in an instant. Before Madigan could stop them, the younger of the two females threw herself over the Mexican's body, pinning him down, while the other woman picked up a large rock and brought it crashing down on his skull with a sickening whack, killing him instantly.

Two of the men were dead, of that there was no doubt. The man that was knocked off his horse when Madigan shot Scar Face was not moving either. Could be playing dead or have the wind knocked out of him, Madigan thought. He rode slowly down toward the man, keeping his rifle at the ready in case of a trick.

Getting closer, he could see where the bullet entered Scar Face's chest. The man laying under him still worried Madigan, though. He turned his horse so that he came around behind the outlaw in case the man might try something. This way the bandit would have to move his dead friend from on top of him to get a clear shot. Madigan wasn't about to take any more chances than he had to.

All the worry was for nothing. As Madigan rode up behind the outlaw, he could see he was no threat to him or anyone else. The bullet that killed his friend had gone all the way through. As Madigan suspected, the second man was trying to pull one of the oldest tricks in the book—drawing his gun while unseen behind another. The Mexican's gun was still gripped tightly in his lifeless hand.

He had leaned down for more cover at the same time Madigan shot through the man in front of him. Madigan's bullet hit him full in the mouth and had blown out the back of his neck. The sight made Madigan sick to his stomach and he gasped for air.

The women were sitting by the man they had killed. As Madigan approached they eyed him suspiciously, but made no move and said nothing.

"You're safe now," he said as he stepped down from his horse and kept a safe distance, for he had witnessed what the women could do. Bending over and keeping an eye on the women, he withdrew a knife from one of the dead men's belts and threw it to them.

"Here, cut yourselves loose. I'll get you something to wear."

The women grabbed the knife and cut each other's bonds. Madigan tried not to look at their nakedness, while at the same time being aware of any threatening moves they made. After cutting themselves free, they just sat there, their eyes following his every move.

To his surprise, the outlaws' horses had stayed where the men dropped. He went over and took the bedrolls from two of them.

"Here, see what you can do with these," he said as he tossed the bedrolls to the women. They gathered the blankets up and with the knife soon fashioned a serape by cutting a hole in the center of each blanket, then pulled it over their heads, tying the sides closed with short strands of rope.

While they were busy clothing themselves, Madigan took a short shovel from his pack to bury the bodies with. As he dug, he still kept a watchful eye on the women, who were now fully covered.

For the first time since he saw them, he realized that they were not Mexicans or Anglos. Their features were different from any he'd seen. They could be Indians, but none that he knew of. Maybe they belonged to a tribe of desert dwellers. Madigan did not know and he didn't plan on finding out; for he would bury the outlaws and be on his way.

The outlaws' horses would carry the women to wherever they wished to go. The horses! A sudden thought struck Madigan. Each horse carried saddlebags and each saddlebag was bulging. What were these men carrying? Did they rob a bank, or maybe a prospector that hit it big? He dropped the shovel and walked to a horse that was grazing beside the trail. The women still watched his every move.

Opening the flap, he was shocked into disbelief. As the sunlight flooded the inside of the bag, he was momentarily blinded by the reflection of gold! Not gold ore or gold nuggets, but hundreds of small gold figurines and utensils!

He quickly checked the other bag and found the same thing. He ran to the next horse, almost scaring it away. Madigan forced himself to stop. Moving slowly, he gained the animal's confidence and was able to check the contents of its saddlebags as well. He could feel his heart pounding in his chest as more gold was uncovered. It couldn't be, but it was! He was breathing hard as the third pair of saddlebags revealed the same treasure. He had to stop to catch his breath. There must be hundreds of thousands of dollars here—all his! He was richer than he ever dreamed of being. The job in California had no meaning now. He could buy the biggest ranch in the state of Texas if he'd a mind to!

Then he remembered the women. They would know about the gold. Maybe it was theirs. Maybe he should kill them. Yes, he could kill and bury them. No one would know. He could melt the gold down and say he made a big strike and smeltered the ore himself. It was done sometimes. No one would care.

His hand went to his gun. Just two quick shots and he would have it all. He would be rich! Rich enough to do whatever he wanted, whenever he wanted. The women seemed to sense what he had in mind. The fear showed in their eyes, yet they remained calm, unmoving.

Then reality hit him. He would not only be rich, he would also be a murderer! The women stood a dozen yards away and for the first time Madigan saw how beautiful they were. They both had silky black hair; the younger one's grew halfway down her back, and the other's was shoulder length. They were both slim, but well developed, with skin that seemed smooth and unblemished, from what Madigan could see under the dirt, unlike most Indians whose skin was burnt dry from the sun and wind.

Then there were their eyes, those beautiful eyes. A man could lose himself in their eyes. And when he looked into the eyes of the younger one a feeling came over him the likes of which he had never felt before.

He also knew they were not afraid anymore. Somehow they knew he was not a man to kill for the sake of gold. Madigan stood there a long while, his mind full of shame for even thinking such a horrible thought.

Madigan instinctively knew the gold figurines belonged to the women, or the women's people, and it meant far more to them than all the gold in the world could to him. He let his gun drop back into its holster. Then quickly, before changing his mind, he took a saddlebag from one of the Mexican's horses and placed it over one of the other saddlebags. This way one horse carried two saddlebags and the other horse carried the third bag. He took the reins, and stooping, gathered up a canteen that fell when Scar Face was shot off his horse. He shook it; it was full. This he placed over the pommel of one of the saddles, then he handed the reins to the women.

"Here," he said with a self-conscious smile.

I must be crazy, he thought. The younger one reached out and took the reins. For a moment their eyes met. This woman, like no other he'd ever known, stirred something within him and he knew he would never be the same again. The older woman said something to her that he could not understand, then turned to Madigan and in a kind of sign language asked him to wait for a moment while she took something from the saddlebag that had belonged to Scar Face.

Many Indians speak both their native tongue as well as English, but prefer to not let on that they understand what is being said. Madigan expected this was how it was with these women, but did not let it show. They had good reason to not trust anyone right now.

What the older woman took from the saddlebag was a little figurine of what looked to him like a man. Unlike the others that he'd seen, it was made out of gold and silver. The figurine was masterfully made, the top half being gold, the bottom being of silver.

She reached for the knife that he'd given her earlier. Madigan quickly stepped back a few paces, not knowing what she was about to do. Both women smiled at his caution. With the knife, the woman pried the little man in half. To his amazement the figurine came apart, not in two pieces, but in three. One part was all gold. The bottom piece was silver, but from the middle came a ring of both silver and gold.

She held this out to him, indicating for Madigan to put it on his finger. He took the ring from her and tried it on. It fit perfectly. Both women placed their hands over his and slowly said what he took to be some kind of a prayer. Then the older of the two took from the top of the figurine a white powder. It came freely into her hand and she pinched some between her fingers and placed it on her tongue, then motioned for him to do the same. Madigan didn't think it could hurt, so he followed suit. Then the women sat down on the ground, and he did the same.

What were these strange women doing? Why had they been captured in the first place? Where'd all the gold come from and where would they take it? There were many questions he wanted to ask but didn't know how. He was torn between his conscience and his need to know. And maybe a little greed.

Madigan awoke from the cold many hours later. The women were gone, along with the gold, but to his surprise the horses were picketed by a small creek a few dozen yards away. He looked down and saw that the ring was still on his finger.

"So it was not a dream," he said aloud. Trying to stand up, he felt light-headed. The powder, he thought.

Judging by the moon overhead, Madigan surmised it was around ten in the evening. He hadn't eaten since morning and his stomach was growling something awful. Looking for a place to build a small fire, he was startled to find that wood was already piled within a small circle of stones. The wood was dry and all he would have to do was strike a match to start it ablaze. Whoever piled the wood had been careful to use wood that would not cause any smoke, although he wasn't worried about anyone seeing it this late at night.

He also noticed that he wasn't in the place where he had been when he first saw the outlaws earlier. Somehow, he'd been moved into a little depression in the earth surrounded by trees. Madigan doubted whether anyone would be able to see the light from the fire either.

He took a slab of bacon from his pack and sliced it into several long strips, then cooked it in his cast-iron skillet along with some beans he'd saved from another meal. He ate until he was full, then spread his blanket out for the night.

In the morning he would try to find some of the answers to the many questions that raced through his mind. While he lay there trying to think, he felt the strangest sensation that he was being watched. Still feeling surprisingly tired for all the sleep he'd gotten, Madigan closed his eyes and drifted off to dreams of golden towns where there was so much gold that plain dirt was valued more.

He had always been an early riser, so at first light he was already drinking a hot cup of coffee. After finishing a second cup, he poured the remaining coffee over the fire, and walked down to the creek to rinse the pot out.

Madigan still felt that he was being watched, but shrugged it off as his imagination. He was in a hurry to get on his way and if, in fact, someone were keeping an eye on him, they would have to move fast to keep up. He planned to make a lot of distance before sundown.

Madigan had just finished saddling up when he heard voices not far away. He lay down in the dirt and inched his way forward through the low bushes until he could see where the sound was coming from. Down on the trail, not a hundred yards below him, were a dozen or more riders. None of them looked friendly, so he stayed hidden as best he could. All but two of the men were on horseback. The two on foot were bent over as they walked, looking for sign. Every few steps they would wave the riders forward. Madigan held his breath as they approached the place where he had buried the three men.

Instinctively, he slipped the thong from the hammer of his Colt, wishing that he'd also brought his rifle with him. To his surprise, the two men walked right over the grave as if it weren't even there!

Why didn't they see the grave, he wondered. He'd made no attempt to hide it. Just dug a single hole for the bodies, rolled them in, then covered it up with dirt and piled rocks on top to keep the animals out. You could hardly miss it on horseback, let alone on foot.

Behind him the buckskin was growing restless and stomped his foot on the hard-packed ground. To Madigan it sounded like cannon fire and he hoped the men below didn't hear it. He lay very still, waiting and watching while the hair on the back of his neck stood on end, every fiber of his being alive. Then the packhorse snorted!

At the sound of the noise, one of the trackers below

looked up. He gave a sign for the other men to do the same. Those on horseback turned to see where the man was looking, and he was looking straight at Madigan! Several men drew their rifles, getting ready for any trouble that might come their way.

Madigan held his breath for what seemed like hours. He dared not move even an eyelid for fear of being seen. Silently he prayed the horses would be still. Then off to his side he caught movement. He could not risk moving, for to do so would surely give himself away to those below. Again Madigan caught movement off to his right, and a little behind him. Had a rider been sent ahead to scout the sides of the trail?

Madigan knew that he must have a plan; his life depended on it. He thought long and hard and decided if the time came, he'd roll to his left while drawing his gun. A quick shot and he would be on his feet and running, then up on the buckskin and he'd ride for the hills. He was bothered by the fact that he might have to leave some of his belongings behind, but better to be alive without them than dead with them.

The movement to his right was getting closer. Madigan tensed, ready for action. More of the men below had drawn their guns. On the count of five he would roll and fire, hoping to surprise whoever it was. He started to count to steady his nerves.

Three, four, he silently counted . . . five. The Colt came easily into his hand and he thumbed the hammer back as he rolled. In one smooth motion he brought the gun up to bear on the target.

The man was crouched down, rifle in hand, trying to find him. His back was toward Madigan, but it was evident what his intentions were. Madigan half-smiled as he watched the man, but he knew that time was running out. If any of the men below got curious, they might ride up to see what was happening. Madigan could not afford to take that chance.

"What are you looking for?" Madigan asked quietly. To his surprise, the man whirled and fired at the sound of his voice. The bullet kicked up dirt less than two feet from where he lay on the ground. Madigan squeezed off a shot. The man was picked up and thrown back from the impact of the bullet. For an instant Madigan started to fire again, but the rifle dropped from the man's grasp as he fell backward, like a tree fallen from a woodsman's ax.

Madigan glimpsed the men below running for cover. In an instant he was up and running while firing another shot in the direction of the men below to make them keep their heads down a little longer. He jumped in the saddle and wheeled the buckskin around so he could grab the pack-horse's rope. The shooting had spooked the animals some and they were both ready to run. He pointed them toward the mountains to the west and gave the buckskin its head. Even though the packhorse's load was light, it was all it could do to keep from holding the big stallion back.

Madigan knew that within a few minutes he would have to bring the buckskin to a walk to let the pack animal rest, and if worse came to worst, he would have to cut the animal loose and let the buckskin carry him to safety. Or he might try another trick. All he would need was a little room between the gunmen and himself.

Looking over his shoulder, he could see no one following. So he brought the horses to a slow gallop to conserve their wind. Ahead of him was a broad plain that appeared to stretch for several miles before it began a climb into the east side of the Rockies. He headed out across it, and glancing back every so often, he soon saw a cloud of dust showing where there was nothing minutes before.

The riders obviously had discovered his escape and were now intent on catching him. A picture flashed through Madigan's mind of a fox being chased by the hounds. The only difference was this fox wore long teeth.

Madigan guessed he must be at least a mile-and-a-half

ahead of the men following behind. A little farther and the horses could get a rest, and if things went well, he would give his pursuers second thoughts.

CHAPTER 2

About three hundred yards ahead of him was a waist-high boulder with a small stand of scrub oak around it. As soon as he saw it, Madigan knew this was the place he was looking for. He rode up and looked the spot over carefully. Seeing that it would do nicely, he dismounted and tied the horses to a tree a few yards behind the large rock. At this point, he couldn't afford to be in a hurry. So he purposely paced himself, not too fast, not too slow. Madigan had a job to do and it would require rock-steady nerves.

From his pack he pulled out a long leather sheath and laid it gently on the ground. Next he felt around for the small tin box that was so carefully packed for just such an occasion. Finding it, he laid it alongside the covered .50-90 Sharps. Madigan carried these to the rock and took the gun out of its sheath.

Madigan had always enjoyed the feel of this heavy buffalo gun, from its polished black walnut stock—fitted perfectly to the massive breech block mechanism with the heavy side hammer to the end of the long barrel with the three steel bands clamping it and the wood forearm together. This was a tool meant for one purpose—to kill at long distances. And this was precisely what he needed now.

Checking the barrel for any obstructions, but finding none, he opened and closed the breech to make sure it worked properly. With the rifle in one hand, Madigan opened the tin box with the other and withdrew a brass cartridge. He forced himself to keep his mind on the job at hand and not the riders that he knew would be coming fast.

The first bullet looked good, so he quickly checked another and then a third. Now it was time to give the men following him the shock of their lives. As he'd guessed, they had closed to about a half a mile, maybe just a little over, but close to the distance he wanted.

Chambering a round, Madigan took off his hat and placed it on the rock in front of him to protect the rifle's finish from getting scratched. Figuring the wind to be about two notches from the north, he adjusted the sights for the distance. Then he held two beads to the left and squeezed off a shot. He was aiming for the leader, but knew if he missed, as he probably would at this range, the bullet would still have a good chance of getting one of the men following behind.

The kick of the rifle set Madigan back for a moment and he had to wait for the smoke to clear before he could see again. But when the smoke cleared, he was greeted with the sight of a clean miss. He chambered another round and was about to pull the trigger when the front rider tumbled out of his saddle. In his haste, Madigan had forgotten how long it took for the heavy bullet to go that distance.

Immediately the rest of the riders turned and raced back to the trees like the very devil was after them. Madigan quickly walked to his pack and grabbed his field glasses to get a better view. To his satisfaction, the man on the ground was not moving. He watched as the others headed for the only cover within reach, the tree line about a quarter-mile back from where the man had fallen.

That the bullet carried enough power to kill at that range was a marvel to him. So maybe another try might just even things up a bit more and, at any rate, it sure couldn't hurt.

Even if the bullet only kicked up dust close to his pursuers, it would scare the hell out of any sensible man. Madigan aimed the big rifle over the area that he saw the riders go into.

Only this time, he held the sights at a point halfway up the trees they were hiding amongst.

He had already killed four men with three bullets, and to hope for another score would be asking a lot. Whether it was curiosity or survival instinct he didn't know, but Madigan was already pulling the trigger before he'd given it much thought.

This time he was ready as the blast knocked him backward. Madigan quickly set the gun down and grabbed his glasses to see where the bullet would hit. To his astonishment, three riders had broken out of the trees at a full run. It was clear that they planned on running him down before he could get mounted and away.

They must have figured that he would shoot once, then try for the mountains a few miles away. The interval it took him to get his glasses was all the time needed for them to believe they were right and that he was riding off. They were wrong, and it cost them dearly. For an instant they rode hell-bent-for-leather, then as if in slow motion the last man jerked sideways in his saddle and slid to the ground.

"Damn," Madigan whispered to himself, "this is a straight-shootin' cannon." Anyway, he wouldn't have to worry about the riders for the moment. The only horse coming toward him was riderless. He waited to make sure they'd given up, at least for the time being. He knew that come nightfall they would ride out and try to get behind him. But as long as they didn't see him leave, they would not take another chance while it was still light.

This close to the mountains it would get dark fairly early. Madigan guessed there were maybe nine hours of usable light left. He wasn't going to take any unnecessary chances, so he took his Winchester out of its scabbard and replaced it with the Sharps. He would keep an eye out for anyone following, and with the Sharps close at hand, he would be ready.

Keeping the small grove of trees between him and his pursuers, Madigan walked the horses due west toward the Rockies, and, he hoped, shelter from his enemies. Every once in a while he would turn in the saddle to see if there was any telltale dust that would give away any riders coming up hard behind him. There was none.

As Madigan rode, he mulled the events of the day over in his mind. He felt no guilt at having to kill, but it did bother him some that he'd been forced to without any say-so in the matter. Now he was forced to run for his life.

Another thought kept entering his mind—the two women and the gold. He couldn't help but think that he was being pulled into this situation by some mysterious force beyond his control.

For now, all he could do was ride along and try to stay alive. He soon rode into the forest at the base of the Rockies, following a trail that turned south by southwest. The trail was rocky and sometimes steep, just wide enough for one horse at a time.

The last hour had been a gradual climb, and Madigan had to rest the horses often. There was still a good six hours of daylight left, but he was aware that he would have to make camp while enough light still remained, as it would be suicide to ride this narrow trail in the dark. He was at least four hours, maybe five, ahead of the gunmen and they would not be able to see any better in the dark than he would.

At the start of the trail he was now on, there were at least two others branching off in other directions. One of these went to a hidden lake a few hours' ride into the mountains, while the other led to a pass much higher than Poncha Pass, which Madigan now rode towards. Unless these men were familiar with the area, they would have to guess where each trail went, and Madigan made sure that he had left no tracks on the trail below for them to follow.

For the moment he relaxed and breathed in the fragrance of the high mountains. The air had a coolness about it, yet it was more refreshing than cold. He pulled the collar of his shirt up over his neck and was soon lost in the splendor of the sights that surrounded him.

As he rode along he whistled and sometimes sang. This was bear country and he didn't want to startle a grizzly. He remembered a mountain man once telling him that unless you were hunting bear, always make some kind of noise to let them know you are there. "Give a bear a chance to get out of your way and you'll likely not be bothered by it," the old trapper told him so long ago.

The trapper also told Madigan that bears seem to have good days and bad days, just like humans. On a good day they run at the first sound from you. On a bad day you could very well end up being the bear's dinner.

"Be prepared for the worst, then when it comes you won't be surprised," the grizzled old mountaineer said. Although the old man of the mountains had given Madigan that advice some ten years past, he still remembered it as though it was yesterday. Another thing the old man mentioned about bears: "Never go into the brush after one. They may be playing you for a sucker, settin' you up for an ambush. No animal can do it better than a big black or grizzly!"

Several times since he started on this trail, Madigan had passed bear sign. Afterward, he would have an uneasy feeling when the trail went around a bend, and the more he thought about what the old-timer said about bears, the louder he whistled. When he tired of whistling, he sang. He was sure the horses were glad when he started to whistle again.

It was getting late, so when a little clearing came into view he decided to make camp. By walking a few feet from camp, Madigan came to an outcropping of rock from which he had a clear view of the valley floor below. He figured he must have come close to fifteen miles since starting up this trail and hoped he could get some much needed rest.

Madigan lifted his binoculars to his eyes and scanned the flats below. A dust cloud marked the passage of the riders on the valley floor far to the east, and Madigan knew they would not dare try to go any further than across the valley until daylight.

Even as he stood watching, the light was fading at an alarming rate. Madigan walked back to camp satisfied that he would be safe for the night. He would trust the buckskin to warn him if any predators got too close. Before retiring, he took the precaution of tossing a rope over a branch and pulling his food pack out of reach of any fur-covered creature of the night. One last cup of coffee and it was time to turn in.

Madigan was up as usual the next morning in time to watch the sunrise in the east. It promised to be a glorious day. If it hadn't been for the wild bunch following him, he would have stopped at the next stream to catch himself a passel of trout. The thought intrigued him, but to stop now meant almost certain death. The fish would have to wait for another time; for now he'd better plan on what he was going to do to get out of the frying pan himself, without getting into the fire.

As soon as the sun got high enough for him to see the valley floor below, he glassed the area thoroughly. About midpoint across the plains below, there was dust rising. So they chose to go but a short distance last night, he thought. They were probably afraid he might try to sneak around behind them. All the better for me, he surmised.

Each time Madigan passed a stream tumbling down into a pool of fresh mountain water, he had thoughts of trout and the fishing trips he and his folks had taken to the mountains around Tennessee. The Tennessee mountains weren't anywhere near the size of the Rockies, but to a seven-year-old they looked mighty big.

He remembered his mother's excitement at the prospect of going for a week into the mountains with him and his father. Madigan's mother was a beautiful woman and would have followed her husband to the edges of hell. And, in fact, did three years later. Madigan would remember the terror of that day for the rest of his life. Sometimes he'd be wakened by the nightmares of what happened so many years before.

His family had been on their way to a new life out West when the Indians struck. It was a terrible thing for a boy to witness, and Madigan could still hear his mother's screams as she kneeled over his father's body as it lay in the dirt where he'd fallen from the Kiowas' arrows. Then the Indians came and took her. There were three of them. They were ugly beasts, painted with war paint and splattered with dried blood, and they smelled of sweat and death. Madigan watched them from the wagon where she had hidden him. After they raped his mother, they cut her throat. He had wanted to cry out but was too afraid, so before they came to the wagon he crept away and hid in the trees. By then it was night and they did not see his tracks.

In the morning he waited to make sure they were gone, then took a shovel and buried his parents in the desolate land where they died. Ashamed of himself for not trying to help them, Madigan made a vow that he would find their murderers and either kill them or be killed trying.

For two days he followed the Kiowa. Hungry and tired, he made himself keep on, not knowing what he would be able to do when he caught them. The renegades did not know they were being followed and made no effort to hide their tracks, while something deep within the boy kept pushing him harder and harder to find these men and make them suffer as much as possible before he killed them.

The Kiowas did not go far—only until they found another wagon to raid. They found liquor and drank themselves unconscious. While they were passed out drunk, Madigan tied each of them to a wheel of the wagon. When they came to, the boy showed each a tintype of his mother and father so that they would know who he was and what he must do.

Then he took a cask of coal oil from the wagon, for it was a peddler's wagon they raided this time, and poured it over the confused men. When he lit the match, the realization of what he was going to do hit the Indians and they struggled to break free from their bonds, but he'd tied them tight and there was no escape for them. The ten-year old boy dropped the flame into a small pool of oil under the wagon, and in a flash the flames engulfed the wagon and Indians together.

Whether or not they screamed he couldn't remember, only that as the fire devoured the men, it also cleansed his soul of the hatred within him, and he lay down and slept for the first time since his parents' death. When he finally awoke, he cried for his mother and father whom he would never see again.

It was then that Madigan heard the noise behind him and turned to face a band of Kiowa braves. There were ten, maybe more. The memory of that day was hazy after all these years, and the number was unimportant. It was easy to see that one was their chief. Madigan expected to die and knew that he was ready. Instead of killing the boy, the braves took him to a town, riding through the night to get there.

Before they turned him loose, the chief said something to the others that Madigan did not understand. One of the braves brought forth a small pouch and took some red powder from it. He then spit in his palm and mixed the powder to a paste. With this he then painted several red stripes across Madigan's cheeks. This done, the Indians rode off in a thundering of hooves and war whoops.

The town was called Bonner Springs because of the springs at the edge of town. He remembered that almost everyone in town had a garden behind their house, and Madigan could still taste in his memory the fresh strawberries and rhubarb pies Aunt Jane would bake every Sunday in the summer. Aunt Jane, as he called her, was the schoolteacher there at Bonner Springs. Of course, she wasn't his real aunt. She'd taken him in the very first day he showed up in town, and she liked him to call her by that name. While Madigan lived with Aunt Jane, she instilled in him the love of reading. And to this day, some twenty years later, he still carried one or two books along with him to read by the campfire at night when he was alone.

Madigan had also found out from one of the old Indian

fighters in town that the paint the Indians put on his face was their way of telling others that he was a brave warrior.

A menacing growl startled Madigan back to his senses. The trail ahead wound through thick brush and fir trees, sometimes growing right up to the edge of the trail. In the middle of the path, standing on his two hind legs, was the biggest grizzly Madigan had ever seen. His right hand edged down toward the Sharps in the saddle boot by his right leg. At the same time he urged the horses back, trying not to make any quick movements that might scare the bear into action.

The bear stood there, his gray-black lips wrinkled back to display large yellow fangs that Madigan could almost feel tearing into his flesh, and three-inch claws still dripping blood testifying to a fresh kill. The bear's coat was a rich brown with tinges of gold where the sunlight fell on it, his head ten feet off the ground. The bear let out a woof from time to time while his little red eyes glared at Madigan as he backed the horses further away, his rifle at the ready. Madigan guessed the brute must weigh close to a thousand pounds, or more.

He felt no desire to kill this magnificent beast, but he was scared and would have no choice if the bear decided to charge. For several minutes Madigan and the brute faced each other. Then without warning the grizzly dropped to all fours and ambled off into the brush beside the trail. Madigan watched, relieved at the confrontation coming to an end. By watching the brush moving, he was able to tell that the bear only went in a few feet from the side of the trail and stopped.

The words of the old mountain man rang in his mind. "Never go into the brush after a bear. They may be playing you for a sucker, settin' you up for an ambush. No animal can do it better than a big black or grizzly bear!" And from the size of this bear, Madigan thought, he must be very good at getting his food!

Not wanting to take any chances by getting too close to

the thicket where the bear was, Madigan scouted his back trail looking for a spot where he could ride around the animal without spooking him into a charge. About a half-mile back, he came to a game trail going up the side of the mountain. Taking his rifle, he set out on foot to see if it would circumvent the bear's hiding place.

After walking for about twenty minutes, he was well above the main trail and could see not only the bear hiding in the bushes below, but a good portion of the trail in either direction. The game path did indeed go well around the bear's hiding place, coming out about a quarter-of-a-mile ahead and around a bend in the trail from the grizzly.

Madigan would have to walk the horses, but it would not be hard for them to move over the path. The hiding place of the bear was backed by a natural rock wall going up to about sixty feet, so he was not worried about the bear coming at him on the game trail.

While walking back to the horses, he chanced to see the sun flash off something metal down the trail in the distance. He stopped and waited, shielding his eyes from the sun to get a better view. The pure mountain air afforded him a clear picture of what was taking place further back down the trail from which he came.

Two riders and four horses were coming fast. They were wearing hats and were fully dressed, so Madigan knew they were not Indians. And he didn't have to be told what the riders were up to. Each man would trail a horse behind him, and when his mount gave out, he would switch to the less tired horse. The Comanches had a name for it. They called it the Death Ride. It enabled a rider to run down someone that was far ahead of him.

So they knew the lay of the land and were hoping to catch him off guard. And they would have too, if it hadn't been for the bear blocking his path. He hurried to get back to the horses. At best he'd only have about an hour, maybe less. But if what he had in mind worked, it would be all the time he needed.

Madigan led the horses up the path, keeping to the edge of the trees and out of sight from the riders coming from below. Finding a place in the trees to hide the horses, he quickly tied them and then hurried back to cover his tracks. At the rate the gunmen were coming, he doubted whether they would see them anyway, but wanted to make sure they didn't.

Next, he returned to the horses and led them on the path above the bear and back to the main trail. Finding a place with some grass, he tied them so they could graze a little. Then he walked back down the path to within a hundred and fifty yards of the bear and waited.

It wasn't long before he could hear them coming. At first it sounded like rocks falling down the side of a rocky hill. Then the sound became more distinct, that of horses' hooves pounding the ground at a fast run. Somehow the riders must have gotten a glimpse of him on the trail ahead of them earlier. The trail twisted and turned so that at times you could see far ahead while at other times you couldn't see more than a hundred feet.

His guess was that they must have caught sight of him just before he stopped for the grizzly. He was almost certain they'd spotted him then or they would not be running the horses as hard as they were. Probably trying to overtake me without warning while I was off guard, he thought. They might have succeeded, too. He didn't think he would have heard them coming if he'd not been expecting their company.

Only blind luck had betrayed them to him, and he wasn't the kind of man to throw an advantage away once he had it. How many times did man live or die because of luck, he wondered. At least today his luck was good and he hoped it would hold for another few minutes. One thing was for sure—he'd know the answer either way.

He was crouched down in the middle of the trail when the horsemen came into view. He came to his feet with the Winchester leveled at them, but he'd no intention of firing unless he was forced to. Shots might be heard by their friends.

And right now he had all the company he wanted.

Seeing Madigan in front of them brought a look of shock from both men. They'd been racing along single file, and as the trail at this point was only wide enough for one horse at a time, they knew that to turn their horses around and flee would be almost certain death. There was only one option open to them.

"Look out!" the first rider yelled as he suddenly saw Madigan in the middle of the trail in front of him. "He's got us covered!"

In less than a heartbeat, they whirled their horses to the right and spurred them into the cover of brush and trees. Madigan almost laughed at the sight of them doing exactly as he had planned. But what he had planned was no laughing matter.

It all happened so fast that the horses didn't get wind of the bear hiding in the brush. In a flash all hell broke loose, starting with a blood-curdling scream, then the two riderless horses breaking out of the underbrush at a full run. Then another scream, followed by the sound of something huge moving fast through the brush. In the next instant the grizzly came charging out into the open, blood dripping from his muzzle, his eyes showing red and fierce. The beast stopped after a few feet and rose up on his hind feet, pawing the air like a punch-drunk boxer, pieces of flesh clinging to his claws.

For a few seconds Madigan and the grizzly faced each other, the bear glaring wildly at the man. Then, like a fighter called back to the ring, the beast was gone out of sight into the brush from which he came. As a stunned Madigan watched, a tremendous growl floated through the air answered by another scream. Then all grew silent except for an occasional grunt from the bear. Madigan had never witnessed anything like this in his life and was dumfounded at what he had just seen.

Then the realization hit him that here he sat out in the open, a mere hundred and fifty yards from a man-killing grizzly. He began to sweat and his mouth felt dry. At that moment he felt very vulnerable. After checking behind him, he quickly covered the distance back to the horses and traded the Winchester for the Sharps. Now, at least if the grizzly charged he would have a gun big enough to give him a fighting chance. Still it was funny how small the Sharps looked in his hands.

Even from this far away he could still hear the bear. After a while he decided to climb a rock to get a better view of the situation. From his position on the rock, Madigan watched the bear leaving a half-hour later, going back down the trail in the opposite direction a short way, then climbing up into the trees above.

Even so, he waited another fifteen minutes before going down to investigate the scene of the attack. He was plenty nervous as he walked toward the clump of trees, and every few steps he would stop and listen for any sounds that might mean the grizzly was returning.

What he saw was a scene from hell. One man was laying up against a tree, his six-gun in his hand, and it looked to Madigan that the cowboy tried to shoot himself before the great beast came back. The man needn't have worried. He bled to death from his extensive wounds before he could get off a shot.

Madigan was not prepared for the sight that greeted him next. The other man lay with his hands up behind his head, just as one might do while getting some rest. From Madigan's position, all he could see was from the middle of the man's chest on up. On a different occasion the cowboy might just be laying there sleeping. But as Madigan stepped around the bush, he grew sick. The bear had fed on the gunman and all that remained was the top third of the body.

Madigan's legs suddenly felt weak and his head swam. All he could think of was getting out of there, so he ran the distance back to the buckskin, who watched his approach with interest. Soon he was galloping up the trail. In a few minutes he returned to his senses.

It is an unwritten law of the West to bury the dead, friend

or foe, and part of Madigan agonized over leaving the bodies
without putting some ground over them. He tried to convince
himself that there was no choice but to leave the bodies, but
a conscience is a powerful thing. So he headed back to do
what was right.

That's when the mountain man's voice came to him again.
"Never stay around where a grizzly has eaten. He's not going
far from his food, and if you mess with it, you just may be his
next meal!" Good advice, Madigan thought as he reined the
horses back around and rode on toward Poncha Pass. As he
rode he looked down at his hands. They were shaking.

CHAPTER 3

Pete LaRue looked down at the body in the dirt at his feet. Gonzales was a tough man to beat with a gun, yet here he lay—dead!

"You men look around for tracks!" he ordered. "Jesus, you put him under the dirt, and the rest of you follow me." Pete LaRue walked quickly to his horse and was soon riding out with eight of his men.

The tracks were easy to follow and from the looks of them, Pete surmised that there were two horses—one being ridden, the other probably a pack animal.

It had taken a while before he and his men chanced leaving the protection of their cover to investigate the hilltop where the shots were heard, giving the man they were after a small head start.

The LaRue men were a wild, unkempt lot. Most were Mexican, some with Indian blood. The rest were an assortment of hard cases brought together by the common bond of men on the run.

Pete LaRue harbored no illusions about his position of being leader. Some men were fast with a gun, others with their fist. Pete LaRue was faster with a gun than most men, and being big and rawboned he could more than hold his own in a fight. But LaRue ruled with a quiet strength, a strength only found in a very few—the few that knew how to use their minds as well as their brawn.

LaRue was smart and knew that vengeance would have to be taken on whoever killed Gonzales, even though he personally knew the man had only been defending his own life. It was the cutthroat code, as long as there were enough men to place the odds heavily in their favor. As LaRue rode he silently prayed his men would lose the trail of the stranger ahead.

The man that shot Gonzales had gotten a twenty minute head start, but with a packhorse in tow, he wouldn't be able to travel very fast.

LaRue and his men rode on in pursuit. At first the trail was easy to follow, but when it went into the trees it became more difficult, so the men had to spread out to find it again. Finally they found where it went out across a high plain toward the distant Rockies to the west.

Looking far in the distance they could see dust rising and knew they were well within a mile of the man they hoped to kill. Jack Lasson was the first to break out of the trees, and was followed closely by Art Simson and a couple of the others.

Pete LaRue knew better than to try to stop them. Jack and Gonzales had ridden together for several years, and if anybody would kill the stranger ahead, it should be him. Pete and the rest followed a short distance behind.

They hadn't gone more than a quarter of a mile when a puff of smoke far ahead caught Pete's attention. The fool's going to waste all his ammunition before we're even in range, he thought. Then he heard the eerie noise, a noise he had heard only once before. In a few seconds Jack was knocked from his saddle.

"A Sharps!" LaRue shouted while spurring his mount back for the cover of the trees. "He's got a Sharps! He can pick us off before we can get within half a mile of him!" he yelled to the other men, who had also retreated to the safety of the trees.

"No man can shoot that well! It's close to half a mile he's shoot'n from!" one of the men hollered back.

"Then what do you think hit Jack?" LaRue asked.

"I don't know, but it wasn't no bullet. Maybe he's just playing dead. Maybe he's afraid of whoever killed Gonzales."

Marty Manning, who on several other occasions had challenged LaRue for leadership, was doing the talking. It made no difference that what he said made no sense. He had the men's attention and that's what he wanted.

"I don't know what's wrong with Jack, but I'm tellin' ya, nobody can shoot and hit anything that far!"

"You ever hear of a Sharps?" LaRue asked disgustedly.

"You mean one of those buffalo guns?"

"That's the one I mean. Just before Jack went down, I heard a noise that I've heard before. It was the sound of a heavy bullet fired from a Sharps! No other sound like it in the world!"

"You sure about that? A rifle can't hit something at that distance!" Manning sneered.

"I'm sure. Of course it would take one hell of a shooter. You saw what it did to Jack out there. I'd say the man at the other end of that rifle knows what it can do and he knows how to use it!" LaRue was nervous and Manning picked it up in the tone of his voice.

"Are you maybe getting too old to lead us? Maybe you want to let this man get away so you won't have to face him!" There was a taunt in Marty's voice, a challenge to LaRue. He antagonized LaRue some more. "I'll show the men what you really are—a coward, afraid to go after one man."

LaRue was angry inside but he let little of it show. He knew from years past that Manning was the real coward and, like scum everywhere, his mouth was bigger than his brains.

"Just how would you handle this situation, Marty?" LaRue asked.

LaRue had taken Manning off guard, and for a long moment Marty was silent.

"He's riding out on us right now as we sit on our butts talking. I'd go after him, that's what I'd do!" Marty turned his horse toward the open plain. "Who's man enough to go with me?" he shouted. Before LaRue could stop them, two other riders answered by kicking their horses out into the open, while Manning followed a short distance behind.

Just like Marty, thought LaRue. Stay in the rear while others put their lives on the line. The thought hadn't left LaRue's mind when off in the distance a puff of smoke told him that the man was still waiting.

"Hit the dirt!" LaRue ordered.

For Marty Manning it was too late. As LaRue and his men watched from their hiding places, Marty was knocked off his horse. LaRue wondered if Marty had known what hit him. The other men yanked their mounts around and raced back to the sanctuary of the trees.

At least LaRue would have no more trouble with Manning, and from the looks of the others, he wouldn't have any problems from them either.

"What do we do now, boss?" one of his men asked sheepishly.

"We wait till dark, then we circle around and try to get the drop on him from behind." LaRue felt in his heart that the man with the long gun would be gone by then. But after just losing two more men to him, he wasn't about to do anything stupid.

"Any of you think you got a better idea?" he challenged. No one replied. "Then make some coffee and beans. We have a long wait ahead of us."

LaRue watched as the men busied themselves getting the camp in shape. What circumstances had brought him to be leading such a bunch of rogues as this, he could only wonder at.

"What about Manning?" someone asked.

"If you want to go out there and get him, be my guest."

"Not me! I don't want to join him," the man said shaking his head.

"Then why'd you ask? Go over there and make some coffee like I told you. When I want you to do something, I'll tell you. Until then, keep your mouth shut!"

LaRue was back in control and he wasn't about to ease up on his men now. That two of them chose to ride out with Manning was a sign to him that he'd been too easy on them. He'd given the men time to think, and when men started thinking, they also started to question their leader's abilities. When that started there could only be trouble. Pete LaRue would not make that mistake again.

After the men had a chance to eat, he called them together. "Here's my plan," he began as they gathered around him. "The way I see it, that man out there has all the advantages. We don't know whether he's still there or not. The later it gets in the day, the more we have the sun in our eyes. We try to ride before dark, and he might just sit out there and pick us off like fish in a barrel."

Several of the men looked out across the high plains. The sun was already low enough on the horizon to force them to shade their eyes. LaRue was quick to pick up on this.

"See what I mean." It was more of a statement than a question. "Now we might wait till dark and then try to get behind him. But I don't think he'll still be there.

"What do you mean, boss?"

"I think he'll be long gone. We can't see him leave because of the sun in our eyes, but he'll have a clear view of us until dark. Our best chance will be to wait for dark, then ride for the mountains. In the morning we can pick up his tracks. Once we do, we'll take the extra horses, and the two best riders can ride him down using the horses in relay." LaRue looked around at his men. They all seemed in agreement.

As LaRue glanced around at the different faces, he again wondered at the circumstances that had brought him to lead such an unruly bunch as the outcasts before him—something he would wonder at many times in the days to come.

"Get some rest!" he ordered. Then he leaned back against a tree to think. How many years had it been it since he felt the comfort of a good meal and warm bed? Or a woman to hold and call his own? Like Mary. How he longed to hold her in his arms, to kiss her and feel her body press against him, to hold her hand as they walked in the moonlight. He could still hear the cheerfulness of her voice when she talked about their plans together.

Her voice . . . the thought brought back the realization that he would not hear her voice ever again. The pain of her death shot through him, and for a minute he felt as if he might weep. He fought hard to hold back the tears. Why did she have to die? She was so young, so beautiful, with a vivaciousness about her he'd never seen in anyone else. His heart ached with the loneliness of her death.

It was still an hour before sunset. LaRue wished it were dark already so he could be on his way again. At times like this when for one reason or another he was forced to mind his time, he was torn with the memories from the past.

He closed his eyes again and drifted back to happier times when his life held promise of better things than cold nights on the trail in the company of rogues and thieves.

LaRue's mother was Irish, big-boned, and blunt in manner, yet gentle in nature. His father often called her a study in contrast. Pete's father was French, a bare-knuckle boxer by trade, but well read in the arts.

Pete could still visualize his father, battered and bruised with a paintbrush in hand, painting the most delicate flowers on a white canvas pulled tight across a frame of his own making.

They were lovers those two, and a gentler pair the Lord never made. But in the ring his father was a killer and his wife sitting in the crowd would not be outshouted by the best of men.

They sent Pete to the finest schools in England and France, where he was a top student learning arithmetic and English, among other things. But Pete's best and most loved subject was archaeology. It was there that he learned of the Aztecs and how they fled their own country with statues of gold and silver.

He studied everything he could about the Aztecs and how

Cortes conquered their land, the country now called Mexico. But what most interested him was the fact that the Aztecs, although grain growers, were the best miners in the world. They worshiped the sun god and made many temples in his honor, and all the temples were covered in gold.

Gold to the Aztecs was as wood is to us. So when Cortes' men took Montezuma's brother-in-law hostage, after Montezuma was killed by one of his own people, they asked for a room full of gold for his return. The Aztecs were quick to reply.

Gold came carried in by great quantities. It was even said that from the mountains a great chain of gold more than a mile in length was being brought to help pay the ransom. Then Cortes' men made a fatal mistake. Fearing a reprisal from the Aztecs once their hierarch was released, they killed him instead. They hoped to keep his death secret, but it was not to be. His death was discovered immediately, and the news went out by runners so that all shipments of precious metal and jewels came to a stop.

The great chain of gold was said to have been dumped in a high mountain lake where only the privileged few of the Aztec priests would know its location. Those slaves that carried it were put to death to keep its hiding place safe from the conquistadors.

But what was of more importance to Pete LaRue was that the Aztecs gathered up all the gold and other precious metals and jewels they could and took them to the north to be hidden against any more invasions by the fair-skinned people that came from the sea.

Pete LaRue searched for years for any documents that might give a clue as to where the Aztec gold was hidden. When he was done with school and returned to New York, he knew as much as any man alive about the Aztec civilization. And LaRue had a pretty good idea where such a people might look to hide their riches.

Many men went down into Mexico in search of the

Aztec wealth, only to find nothing. LaRue was sure the gold and silver were not in Mexico any longer. It was his educated guess that fearing more attacks from the conquistadors, the Aztecs took as much of their wealth as a thousand men could carry and crossed into the Colorado Territory somewhere west of the Continental Divide, and not too far, maybe twenty-five miles or so, from the town of Durango, or maybe even a little south into New Mexico. But LaRue was sure it was somewhere in the general location of Durango.

To further strengthen his theory were the legends told by the Indians of the Southwest, about many men in strange dress carrying baskets full of gold into the mountains of Colorado. It was there that these strange people moved into dwellings upon the cliffs that were built years before their arrival by an ancient race of grain growers. Here the Aztecs lived for many years until they all disappeared one night, taking all evidence of their visit with them, just like the old ones before them, never to be seen again.

The Indians of this area would not go near the cliff dwellings for fear of the evil spirits they believed to be there, nor would they show any white men the way.

It was in this area that LaRue concentrated his search for the hidden treasure. He knew that if he could find the mysterious dwellings of the ancient people, the gold should be close by.

Another problem to deal with was that this land was the home of the Ute, Navajo, and roaming bands of Apaches. Any man caught out in the open was sure to be tortured to death.

LaRue spent many years searching for these mysterious houses built on the side of the cliffs, hiding by day and searching by the light of the moon when the Indians were in their camps, but to no avail.

Then one night as he was returning to camp, he came

across a prospector with an arrow in him. Dying, the man told of finding the abode of the long lost people. He was able to tell LaRue of its general whereabouts, but with a warning: "Do not go searching for it alone!"

Before the old man died, he held out his hand and to LaRue's amazement, in it was a little gold figurine. One other thing got LaRue's attention: the arrow that killed the old prospector had a point made of gold hardened with silver.

Now the gold fever caught hold of Pete LaRue like the lure a beautiful woman holds some men against their will. For hours he would sit and look at the small figurine, almost willing it to give up its secrets. He soon grew slim from not taking the time to eat. At the end of a month he looked haggard and unkempt; his mind drifted and he could not remember from one day to the next.

Finally out of his mind with fever, he wandered from his hiding place out into the desert to die, the figurine clutched in his hand. The Utes found him there lying in the sand, clothes torn from his body. They found him there talking to himself, yet they let him live.

With some Indians there is a belief that the spirit of the one you kill becomes part of your own. It makes you stronger, so they believe. To kill one that is out-of-his-head crazy is to make your own spirit weak, but to help that person is big medicine.

So they took Pete LaRue to a cabin built in the rocks with only one way in. It went unseen except by a very few for many years. LaRue had once passed only yards from its entrance on one of his searches and hadn't seen it. The Utes took him there but would go no closer than fifty feet from the cabin. Then they left leaving Pete to go the rest of the way on his own.

Even in the most shattered of minds, there is an instinct for survival, and Pete LaRue found his way into the cabin. There he found tins of food to eat and a small spring in back of the cabin that gave up clear, sparkling water. Under the cot he found clothes. It was obviously the cabin of the old prospector.

In a few days his mind again grew calm. Having found himself at death's door and surviving, Pete LaRue again became the thinker he once was. And for the next few weeks, while he got his strength back, he planned on how to find the treasure he was looking for.

The first thing he realized was that it would take help in getting the gold, and that meant he would have to be able to make a payroll. Since he was penniless, that left only one avenue open to him: he would have to give up a share of whatever he found. LaRue also knew he would only get two kinds of men for a proposition like that: prospectors, who usually liked to work alone and would, if given the chance, strike out by themselves; the second choice was to hire a gang of drifters and outcasts.

The sound of a coffee pot being dropped snapped LaRue back to the present.

The men were starting to move about, getting restless at having to wait, and anxious to be on their way again.

The sun was setting in the west, giving just enough light to see by. From where Pete sat he could see the men were already saddled and ready to move.

His eyes jumped from one man to the next, analyzing, then dismissing each man in turn. Now that Manning was gone, he would have little trouble with them.

Someone had saddled LaRue's horse for him, so all that was needed was to mount up and be on the way. Pete pulled himself erect and walked stiffly to his horse. The men waited for him before riding off toward the distance unknown.

"What do you want us to do, Pete?" Shorty asked as LaRue rode past.

LaRue thought for a moment. "Just fan out. Everyone pick his own trail. It will be harder to see us if we're all spread out than if we're in one big bunch. A couple of you men find the bodies and bury them!" It felt good to be giving orders again without any questions from the likes of Manning.

In silence, the men formed a long skirmish line in the dark. LaRue rode several yards in front with his friend Shorty beside him.

Shorty was the only man other than LaRue that was not an out-and-out cutthroat. He'd been a teacher in a boys' school back East. He was of mild yet firm manners, and came West to get a little excitement, he said.

One would think Shorty would be timid at the sight of a gun, since he had never fired one before coming out West. Nothing could be further from the truth, for Shorty took to firearms like a duck takes to water. And he was more than just a good shot. His speed and shooting was held in awe even by the most accomplished gunslinger. Even the late Marty Manning was afraid to upset him.

Marty once told LaRue of having seen a top gunslinger tease Shorty until all the men in the bar were in hysterics. Then after Shorty called him a bastard, which he probably was, the gunslinger told him to draw, at the same time going for his own gun. Shorty drew and fired twice before the man cleared leather. Each shot hit true, and the man slumped to the floor dead before he knew what hit him.

When asked how he became so proficient with a gun, Shorty would answer, "As near as I can figure, it was a quirk of nature, as I never practiced even once." LaRue was glad this little, mild-mannered schoolteacher was indeed his friend.

Ahead lay the dark outline of the Rockies with Poncha Pass somewhere to the south. LaRue was familiar with the area and figured that the stranger ahead would undoubtedly head for the Poncha.

It was from the head of the trail leading to the pass that LaRue would send two of his men with extra horses to run the stranger down. Already the stranger had cost LaRue and his bunch dearly, both in time and men. But LaRue still secretly hoped he would get away.

The air was cool as they rode through the night, each man lost in his own thoughts. LaRue's mind drifted back once again to the past. Many months had come and gone since the Indians saved his life. After regaining his strength he made his way south to Sonora and enlisted the help of every cutthroat and saddle tramp he could find, amongst them Marty, whom he had known before. At least now LaRue was rid of him and his problems.

"Why are we chasing this man?" Shorty asked. The question took LaRue by surprise.

"He killed Gonzales. Why else would we track a man halfway across hell's half-acre?"

"Seems to me that losing two more men to a man that Gonzales would have killed, if he hadn't been killed first, is a bit much to pay, isn't it?"

"You and I know that, but the others live by the emotion of the moment, not by logic or common sense. As long as we're going in the same direction as the man we're after, I'll let them have their vengeance."

"Still doesn't make much sense to me. Could get more of us killed and for what? Would have done the same thing myself if Gonzales was sneaking up on me like that!"

Pete LaRue turned in his saddle. "Shorty, you and me, we both know that it was self-defense on the stranger's part. But those men out there don't think like you and me. They like killin' and stealin'. It's a way of life to them. Hell, none of them can even write, let alone read. They live their lives from one miserable day to the next. Most are cowards hiding behind their guns. That's why they're afraid of us. We're faster than them and they know it. And we are their only hope at the moment to get something out of life, other than a bullet someday."

"I see what you mean. How do you think they will be once we find the treasure?"

Pete smiled at his friend. "I wouldn't turn my back on any of them."

First light found the men at the trailhead to Poncha Pass. The two best riders were getting ready for the ride ahead.

The rest of the men were looking for sign. There was a coolness in the air promising the threat of snow at the higher elevations.

"Not a thing to show anybody even came this way at all," one of the men said as he scanned the vast plains they had just come across. "Don't suppose he just laid up last night and let us go by in the dark, do you?"

"Not much chance of that. He'd be taking too big a chance that we might come up on him without him seeing us. No, he's gone on up the pass somewhere. There was a stiff wind last night that covered his tracks, that's all."

"What makes you so sure he didn't take one of these other trails?"

"Because the boss knows this part of the country and he says the man went this way!" Shorty said with a warning to his voice. "Anybody want to argue about it can step right up and start in. But they'll have to do it with me and I'm cranky from lack of sleep right now!"

"No harm meant, Shorty. We was just askin', that's all."

Shorty turned so that only LaRue could see his face and winked. Soon the two men were ready to ride.

"Leave most of your stuff with us so you'll be as light as possible. Take only one rifle in case you can get a clear shot at him, but shoot only if you're sure you can hit him the first time. Otherwise you'll give yourselves away and he can take cover and pick you off before you can get close.

"If you don't have any questions then, get crackin'! We'll wait a while so as not to stir up any more dust than we have to. Good luck, men." LaRue waved them on and within a few minutes they were out of sight. As LaRue watched them ride away, a strange sadness welled up inside him—not for them, but for the man they were going to kill.

An hour after the two riders left on their hunt for the stranger, Pete LaRue moved the rest of the men ahead. It would be hours before the men could even hope to catch up and surprise the lone man with the big rifle.

The trail took a steady climb through some of the most beautiful country LaRue had been through in a long time. The rest of the men were strung out behind him, as the path would only allow one rider at a time along most of its narrow ledge. From time to time the men could get a look at the valley below them from which they came. It was good that he'd moved the men fast enough across the plain below so as to raise some dust. He hoped it would afford the stranger a warning that they were coming.

In his heart Pete LaRue wished to be done with this whole affair, the gold included. It'd taken him weeks to round up enough men to get the job done that he had in mind. Now, after weeks of being away, it all seemed like a bad dream from the distant past.

As Pete rode along he wondered if he was doing the right thing. Maybe the little gold figurine was the only one of its kind and there was no other Aztec gold to be found. Too late now, he thought. He had cast his destiny and entrusted his future to the low-life that was trailing along with him.

Even if there is gold and they find it, it would not be an easy task to keep it out of the hands of the men. Men like these would not be content for only a share, no matter how large it might be. These are greedy men of no proper upbringing, and honor of one's word means nothing to them.

At the next widening of the trail, Shorty rode up beside Pete. "From that look on your face I'd say you were thinking mighty hard about something. Anything you can talk about?"

"Just thinking," LaRue started, "just thinking that if I had it to do over again I would have kept the figurine and been satisfied."

"I was wondering if that might be it. You don't have to worry about me. Find gold or not, I have what I want—freedom to go where I please, when I please." Shorty lowered his voice so as not be be overheard by the others. "Another thing that you should know. When and if the time comes that you need someone to stand beside you against these fellows back here, I'll be there. You can count on it!"

Pete looked over at his friend and nodded his head. "Thanks," he replied.

Around four o'clock, as they were riding over a ridge, one of the men came forward and pointed toward the sky ahead.

"Looks like something's dead or dying up ahead. Them buzzards don't circle like that unless they're getting ready for a meal."

"How far off you make it?" LaRue asked.

"Three, maybe four miles at the most. Want me and some of the men to ride on up ahead and check it out? Maybe our men got that bastard and now the birds are waiting for them to leave so they can get to eatin'."

"Go on up if you want, but don't stray further than you have to. And keep an eye out for a good place to make camp. Be getting dark in a few hours."

Several of the men rode on ahead and were soon lost from sight over the next ridge. LaRue and the rest rode at an easy pace. They were in no hurry to stir up any more dust than necessary. It wasn't long before they came upon one of their riders sitting along the trail.

"Where's the others that rode up with you?" LaRue asked.

The man said nothing, just flicked his thumb in the direction of the trail ahead. In a minute LaRue dismounted alongside the other men who'd gone on ahead to see what the buzzards were about.

"Over there," one of the men said waving toward some thick brush. Pete walked a dozen feet before he was greeted with a sight that made his stomach crawl. The partly-eaten bodies of the two riders he sent on ahead were laying together where they'd been dragged by the bear.

"That bear might still be around close, so keep your eyes open. Not likely he'll leave his dinner this soon. Must've scared him off when you came riding up," LaRue said. The men looked around nervously, not wanting to meet the same fate as their friends.

"Get them buried and let's get out of here before it comes back for a try at the rest of us," LaRue said as he walked back to his horse. "The rest of you men that aren't digging the graves, get your rifles and stand guard. Anybody seen the horses?"

"They weren't here when we found the bodies. The bear must have scared them clean into the next territory! Be lucky if we ever see them again."

The bear watched from cover high on the hill above the men. He was content to just watch. His belly was full.

CHAPTER 4

The events of the morning had unsettled Madigan. He wanted no more of this game that he had been drawn into through no fault of his own. When he planned the destruction of the two riders that were following him, it almost seemed as a joke in his mind. Now after witnessing the brutality of the bear's attack, it was as if a terrible sickness had overcome him.

Madigan felt a guilt that transcended his very soul. To say he was remorseful would be to understate the way he felt by tenfold. But it was over and done and his hope was that he was also done with the men trying to kill him. Being a survivor first, Madigan knew that he could and most probably would kill again to protect himself from being killed.

The buckskin beneath Madigan carried him strong and sure along the narrow trail as it ran along, first through forest of majestic pine and fir, then dropping here and there to a cool meadow of high mountain grass where he would stop to let the animals graze and gather their strength for the never-ending climb ahead.

On the occasions when he stopped to let the horses rest, it was always at the far side of the meadow, right at the tree line so as to be able to duck out of sight at the first sign of trouble. He only picked the meadows large enough to afford him a long-range shot but would be too great a distance for anyone except another man with a Sharps. Madigan had very little fear of falling prey to any of the men that dogged his back trail, for had they been in possession of a long-range rifle, they would have turned it on him while he was still on the high plain.

He even dozed while the horses munched on the sweet, green grass around him, for the big buckskin was always vigilant and would warn him long before any danger got close. He also thought of the girl with the long, black hair and when he did so, he'd get a stirring within him that made him very uncomfortable.

So it went for the next few days. By the time he reached Poncha Pass on the morning of the third day, he had almost put the outlaws out of his mind, but having been a scout and Indian fighter, Madigan never really allowed himself to forget completely. To forget would be to bring almost certain death upon himself.

Still the days were bright and the air was clear and cool, quite a contrast to the valleys and plains far below, and he enjoyed just riding along daydreaming of the dark-haired girl and the ranch he hoped to someday own.

Madigan was riding along enjoying the scenery when something, a hunch or impulse if you will, caused him to turn around in his saddle. At first he was not sure if he had seen the flash on the mountain above him or had just imagined it. He watched for a while longer, but to no avail, so he dismissed it from his mind. Sometimes in the clear mountain air the sun will catch the wings of an eagle in flight, and although one cannot see the bird, the reflection can be, and is, quite bright. Yet, his instincts told him to check again to make sure.

He crossed Poncha Pass early in the morning and would cross the San Luis River sometime the next day if he was lucky, but Madigan wasn't in much of a hurry. He enjoyed being alone in the wilderness and wasn't looking forward to getting back to civilization any sooner than he needed to.

When he reached the San Luis, he planned to camp a day or two and get a belly full of fish. He no longer feared the men that had been following him as he hadn't seen hide nor hair of them since the bear attack. There might be a few Indians around, but most of them were plains Indians and didn't get into the mountains much except to hunt once in a while. Just the same, he'd keep an eye out for any trouble headed his way, but Madigan was sure that for the next few nights he would get some pretty good sleeping done.

Several times he lingered along a stream or grassy meadow, breathing in the vastness between the Rockies and the Great Divide. So when night fell he was not as far as he had planned to be and made camp along a fast-running stream whose noise drowned out all other sounds around him. If not for being so tired as he was, he would not have picked this spot, but would have moved to quieter ground where he might have been warned of approaching danger.

Madigan must have been more tired than he thought, for he made other mistakes that he would not ordinarily make. One was to leave his Colt hanging on a branch a few feet away instead of under his blanket as he normally did. He also didn't bother to remove the Sharps from the scabbard by the saddle. Neither gun was far away, just out of reach if he needed them in a hurry.

Yet living as Madigan did, even in his fatigue, he still took some precautions. So it was as he drifted off to deep slumber, a slumber that he might not wake up from.

As far as he could tell it must have been around two in the morning when he awoke with a start. There in the light of the moon stood two forms. One held the Sharps. And it was pointed straight at Madigan's head!

"So the sleepy one is awake. What will he do now, this man called Madigan?"

Madigan took a deep breath and let his vision clear so that he could see the outline of the man who was talking to him.

"You know me?" he asked, trying to peer into the darkness to see if there were others hidden in the shadows. He could see no one else.

"Yes, I know you. I wasn't sure till I found the Sharps, but now I'm sure. You're the bastard Captain Sam Madigan from the U.S. Cavalry."

"What do you want?" Madigan asked while keeping an eye on the other man.

"Nothing special. I'm just gonna kill you and leave your bones to rot. I always wanted a Sharps and now it seems as if I have found one for my own." The man opened the breech and found the rifle unloaded.

"Where do you keep the bullets for this cannon?" he asked irritably. There was something familiar about the intruder's voice. Then it hit Madigan like a bomb! It was Harry O'Neill! It took all Madigan had to control his anger.

"Over in the pack, in a little tin box, but you'll never get to use them," he said. "It takes a man to shoot a Sharps. All I see is a big-mouthed rat!" Madigan was hoping for more time to figure out his plan of action. O'Neill stared at him for a moment, then turned to his companion and smiled.

"You keep an eye on him while I get the bullets for this here gun." He raised the rifle for emphasis. "I want to find out how big a hole it will make in this bastard's head!"

Madigan needed to act fast. He waited for O'Neill to go over to where his pack lay, then when O'Neill was busy digging around for the ammunition, Madigan made his play. In one motion he kicked the blanket off and levered a round into the Winchester he had hidden beside him. At the same instant, the guard, realizing what Madigan was up to, went for his side arm. Madigan was a split-second faster, and his bullet hit home while the man's gun had barely cleared leather.

Even as the man fell backward, Madigan was off and running, firing a shot in O'Neill's direction. Madigan expected O'Neill to fire back, but to his surprise, O'Neill dropped the Sharps and bolted for the shadows. Madigan fired a couple more rounds after O'Neill as he ran through the trees. But not being able to see in the dark of the forest, Madigan stumbled headlong into a tree, giving his rifle a good whack in the process. It jammed before he could get off another shot. He apparently had missed O'Neill anyway, and was not surprised to hear him ride out on a dead run. Madigan quickly gathered up his Colt and then checked to see that the Sharps was all right. It had fallen on the pack and wasn't hurt.

The man he had shot lay on the ground where he had fallen, groaning softly. Madigan kicked the man's gun away, then put the barrel of his Colt to the man's head. The man's eyes opened slowly and Madigan could see the man was no threat, as it was plain to see that he would soon die.

"Who are you?" Madigan asked. The man looked up with a hatred in his eye that Madigan had seen in but few men.

"My name is Rodino and you have killed me."

"You could have kept on riding. Nobody said you had to come into my camp," Madigan said. "I was defending my life, so I have no remorse in killing you," he added.

The man lay quiet for a moment as though thinking something over, then half-smiled and coughed up a little blood. "You are the man called Madigan, the hunter of men, aren't you?"

"That's what they call me," Madigan affirmed. "Why were you wanting to attack me? Have I done anything to you or your kin to cause you to want to kill me?"

The dying man tried to sit up but did not have the strength, so Madigan helped him, pulling his saddle behind the man's back for support while they talked.

"Thanks," the dying man said, and Madigan noticed the hatred had left the man's eyes, replaced with sadness. "You have done nothing to me or my kin."

The young cowboy then said, "I am dying—that I am sure. Before I go, I will try to tell you some things that might save you from the same fate."

"Why would you want to do that? I have shot you, so why help me now?" Madigan asked. The man held out his hand motioning Madigan to take it.

"Because you are everything that I wanted to be and am not. I give you my hand and my word so you will know that what I tell you is true."

Madigan took the cowboy's hand in his, and at that moment wished that he had known this man under different circumstances. "What is it you want to tell me?" he asked. The cowboy drew in a deep breath, then began his story.

"The man you just ran off is no friend of mine. I was only tagging along for what I hoped would be enough money to buy a small ranch somewhere." He coughed and a little blood ran down his chin. Madigan took his kerchief and wiped it off.

"Thanks," the cowboy said with a look of sorrow. "I guess I came into it about three days ago down in Maysville. I'd been doing some prospecting and had come to the end of my grub, and had no money to buy any more."

"I've been there myself a few times," Madigan admitted.

The cowboy managed a knowing little laugh, then began again, his voice sometimes barely a whisper. "Like I said, I was out of money and I was hungry, so I went to Maysville to try to get a grub stake when I ran into this hombre named O'Neill. He offered me a drink, so I took him up on it. One drink led to another, and before you know it, he was tellin' me a story about saddlebags full of little gold statues and how if I helped him we'd both be rich." Another cough, more blood. Madigan gave him a little water from the canteen and adjusted the cowboy's head so he could be more comfortable.

"Sounds funny, don't it? A full-grown man like me, fallin' for a fool story like that. But I did—hook, line, and sinker."

"Doesn't sound so silly to me," Madigan said, thinking of the saddlebags of gold, his curiosity suddenly aroused.

"Anyway, this O'Neill says that he and five others were runnin' from the law and headed into the mountains northeast of Durango when they chanced to come upon some Indians having themselves a ceremony of some kind."

"Did he say what kind of Indians they were?" Madigan asked.

"Didn't know what they were. Just said they were different from any redskins he ever saw before."

"What were they doing?"

"O'Neill said they were about seventy-five in number, maybe fifty of them were what he took to be warriors. The rest, and this is the funny part, were women, all dancing around this huge fire, and none of them had any clothes on. Kind of stupid to believe such a story, wasn't it?" the cowboy said, emotion filling his voice. "I guess it was more stupid to die for something like that, but that's what I'm doing."

"Maybe there was more truth to the story than you think."

"Well, if you're Sam Madigan, I guess you'd know better than me about that."

"What do you mean?"

"O'Neill said that these women were a dancing all around, beautiful women too, or so he said. Then one of his men spotted a small mound to the side of the fire. Do you know what was on the mound?"

"Let me guess. Piles of gold?"

"Close. On the mound was a large statue in gold and all around its base was thousands of smaller ones also in gold. O'Neill told me that he and his men decided right then and there to take the gold for themselves. Their plan was a simple one. Ride in with their guns a blazin', grab the gold, and run for it.

"By the time they got set to attack, all the warriors were so busy watchin' the women that O'Neill and his men were able to walk their horses right up to them before they were even seen."

"Didn't the Indians try to stop them?" Madigan asked.

"They tried, but against six-guns and with surprise on O'Neill's side, it was all over in a minute. While the Indians were trying to take cover, a couple of the men had enough time to fill some saddlebags with the small gold statues and ride out again. The Indians, after regrouping, killed a couple of men that got greedy and tried for some more gold. Anyway, that's the story O'Neill told me. One other thing, he also said they grabbed two of the women and planned to make them tell where the gold had come from," the cowboy said in a failing voice.

By now it was plain to see the young cowboy was just about gone, as his breathing was shallow and he coughed every few words. But he forced himself to go on and Madigan listened.

"Where did he say he had all this gold that he and his men stole from those Indians?" The man looked up, a look of amusement on his face.

"He said you have it!"

"Me?! Why would he think that?" Madigan tried to look astonished at his statement, remembering full well the two naked women and the saddlebags full of gold.

"O'Neill said he and the rest of his men were bringing the gold to Denver to change it for money. They planned to melt it down so it looked like it had been smeltered, then sell it to the Denver mint."

"Why would they bring it all the way to Denver through the mountains when there were other places much closer to where they started?"

"They didn't have much choice. They were wanted men, so they couldn't go west without taking a chance of being arrested," the cowboy answered.

"How did I get involved in this story of his?" Madigan asked, curious at the answer.

"O'Neill said they had crossed over the Rockies and were just through crossing a high plain with the women in tow, still naked he said, but who would believe that, when he had to make water while the others rode on ahead. Just as he was catching up to them, he heard firing and saw two men fall. He took to cover and said he saw you ride out and even though the last man had his hands in the air, said you shot him too!"

"Sounds like something O'Neill would concoct up," Madigan said. "Then what was I supposed to do?" Madigan asked with tightened jaws.

"He said you raped the women and then shot them and left the bodies there to the wolves while you rode off with the gold. He said it took him close to four hours to bury everybody or he would have come after you right away. By then it was too late and he lost your trail, so he headed back to get help." Madigan looked at the man in silence for a while, wondering why he bothered to tell him all this.

"And you believed him? I mean, that I killed all of them and took the gold?"

"At first I might have, then he told me he knew who you were. After he told me you were Sam Madigan, the scout, the one they call the man hunter, I began to doubt him. Figured he had another reason to blame you."

"With a far-fetched story like that, how did you believe any of it in the first place?" Madigan questioned, irritation showing in his voice.

The cowboy slowly reached into his pants pocket and retrieved a small gold figurine. "Because of this! He had half a saddlebag full of these. When you've been hungry for a few weeks your mind does funny things, and at the time I would have followed him to hell and back." He moved his right hand to the wound in his chest. "I guess you might say I did follow him to hell, but it doesn't look like I'm coming back, does it?"

He took the little gold man in his hand and turned it over and over as he talked. "Is there any truth to O'Neill's story?" the wounded man asked.

"Some. But I didn't kill the women or anybody that had their hands up. And I didn't take the gold. I gave it back to the women, although I often ask myself why. You, my friend, have died in vain, for I have nothing except a few guns and some supplies that would have interested O'Neill or anyone else."

"I had so many plans and now I'm dead," the cowboy said with remorse.

Before the cowboy died, he asked Madigan to bury him away from the stream. "Too many animals come down to drink and I don't want to be their dinner," he had said. He also gave Madigan the little gold man.

Madigan buried him there on a little knoll back from the stream, then piled stones over him and cut a rough cross for his grave.

The next day Madigan left the cowboy there and rode out toward the Great Divide and a future of uncertainty. But one thing he took to heart: if he ever came across O'Neill he would kill him without mercy, not only for what O'Neill had done to Madigan so many weeks before, but for this boy that needlessly lay buried beneath the ground.

Madigan skipped breakfast as usual, so later in the day, when the sun was high overhead, he stopped by a small creek and dropped in a line. No sooner had his bait hit the water then a hungry trout took the hook and the fight was on.

Madigan played with him for a while then, when the fish tired, pulled him in. He was just reaching to pull the trout out of the creek when, in the water's reflection, he saw a flash of light high overhead on the mountainside in front of him. If he had not been looking into the water he would have missed it altogether. He quickly looked up but could see nothing. This time he was sure it was not the reflection from an eagle's wings. It was a flash from something metal.

CHAPTER 5

O'Neill kept riding until he was sure he was safe from the man he had planned to kill. Now, in the quiet of the night, he took his scarf and pressed it against the fresh wound on his face. It was bleeding badly and it took some time before he got the flow of blood stopped. Another inch to the left and he would not be alive, but he was. And he was determined to make Madigan pay for this mark he'd be forced to wear for the rest of his life.

It didn't matter that O'Neill had brought it on himself, for cowards such as he never took the blame when due. All that mattered was that someday, somewhere, he'd put a bullet in the back of the man who had done this to him.

That his friend died did not bother him in the least. He had planned on killing him anyway after he got what he wanted, so he felt no loss. Except, of course, now he would have to find another to take his place.

O'Neill got down from his horse and, not bothering to unsaddle, tied him to the branch of a tree. He then curled up in his blanket and went to sleep, leaving his horse to dry in its own sweat. Morning found him stiff and sore, the left side of his face caked with blood. He was hungry and scared, for he had never spent much time in the mountains alone, even while he was in the army, always preferring to surround himself with others for protection. He pulled his watch from his pocket with trembling hands and realized that he had slept till mid-morning. O'Neill cussed at his luck. "Should have shot that bastard Madigan when I had the chance," he mumbled to himself.

Later in the day, after constantly looking over his shoulder, O'Neill saw the smoke from a campfire ahead of him. Reasoning that it couldn't be Madigan, he stopped long enough to pull the dried scab from his face. After making sure there was plenty of fresh blood, he laid over in his saddle and started towards the camp.

"Rider coming in!" someone yelled. O'Neill slumped over in the saddle, closed his eyes, and let his horse lead him in. In a few seconds he heard footsteps running toward him. He took a deep breath and leaned over still further until he fell to the ground.

"He's hurt! He's covered with blood! Get him over to the fire!" a voice commanded.

O'Neill kept his eyes closed, feigning unconsciousness. It worked, and soon he was being carried to where several blankets had been placed on the ground.

"Put him down gently, boys. No tellin' how bad he's hurt," LaRue ordered.

"Water, I need water," O'Neill moaned through half-closed lips. A man brought a canteen over and held it to his mouth.

"Not too much at first," the man said. "Just take it easy for a while. We'll take care of you."

O'Neill opened his eyes enough to see that the man who brought him water was not much taller than a young boy. He started to laugh but stopped himself in time, making it seem like a cough instead, but not before Shorty caught the beginnings of the laugh and became instantly suspicious of the stranger before him.

"I'll get you something to eat. Try not to move," Shorty said as he stepped away and moved toward the fire-blackened cook pot full of beans. "Stir those beans up and give the wounded man some. He looks hungry," Shorty ordered the cook.

LaRue stood back watching the whole affair as Shorty came toward him. He noticed Shorty loosen the thong from his Colt as he came closer.

"What's up?" he asked as his friend walked over.

"It's that wounded man. I get an uneasy feeling when I'm close to him. Maybe it's me, but I think he's trying to pull the wool over our eyes."

"Why do you think he'd do that?"

Shorty looked around uneasily before speaking. "Maybe he's got friends hid out waiting to catch us off guard. Maybe he's a friend of the guy we had the run-in with a few days ago. I don't know, but he just doesn't look like he's in as bad a shape as he's putting on."

LaRue shifted his weight to his left foot. "I'll go have a chat with him. Might find out what he's up to. Quietly spread the word for everybody to be on guard just in case."

O'Neill watched as LaRue crossed over to where he was laying.

"This your bunch?" he asked as LaRue crouched down beside him.

"I hired them, if that's what you mean." Pete shifted his weight to the other leg. "Where'd you get that wound, if you don't mind me asking."

O'Neill didn't mind at all. In fact, he was waiting for someone to ask so he could exercise the plan he had dreamed up just minutes before. If everything went the way he hoped it would, he'd have all the men he needed and at no expense to himself.

"Don't mind at all. Just lucky to be alive!"

"Who did that to you?"

O'Neill shifted around trying to get comfortable, letting out little moaning sounds as he did so.

"It's kind of a long story. Are you sure you want to hear it?" LaRue nodded his head. "It happened about five days ago, give or take a day or two. I was riding along just minding my own business when I heard some screaming in the distance.

Spurring my horse on at a fast run, I came upon some men—there were about five of them—raping a couple of Injun women."

O'Neill stopped to let what he had said sink in. By now several other men had gathered around. "I ordered them to stop. But instead of stopping they started shooting at me! I drew and shot back getting three of them before I was forced to run for cover.

"Now I ain't an Injun lover, but what them boys was doing to those women wasn't called for, Injun or not! So I couldn't just leave them. I started to reload my side arm when one of them boys rushed me and I had to fight him barehanded. It was a terrible fight. All the time I was worried that the other man might sneak up behind me and shoot me while I was unarmed." O'Neill glanced around at the faces above him. He knew he had them hooked. "Those kind will do that, you know."

"Do what?" Shorty asked.

"Why, sneak up and shoot you in the back, that's what. Course, don't expect someone like you to know that, but it's the gospel."

"What are you implying, 'someone like me'?" Shorty was starting to boil and several of the men stepped back to give him room.

"Why look at you, boy! You're not much bigger than a child. Couldn't put up much of a fight against a real man now, could you?"

LaRue saw what was coming and put his hand on Shorty's shoulder. "He's half out of his head, Shorty. Doesn't know what he's talking about. Better you go over and have some beans while you cool off." Shorty eyed his friend for a moment, then turned his back and ambled off.

"You shouldn't talk to him like that. He can kill you before you can slap leather any day of the year."

"That pip-squeak? Who says—him?" O'Neill said with a sneer.

"No, the men he killed and there have been plenty of them. So for your own safety, keep a civil tongue in your head when you're around him. Now tell us the rest of your story," LaRue demanded angrily.

"I finally got the best of him and was able to grab his gun and put a couple bullets in him before the other one could get behind me. Diving for cover, I was just in time to see the other one ride out. I cut the women loose and buried the men, only decent thing to do. After I was done, one of the women came up to me and gave me something."

O'Neill reached into his pocket and retrieved a little gold figurine. The men gasped as they saw it. "She told me that her tribe had thousands of these and I could have as many as I wanted. Only one problem. An enemy tribe had captured her people and now held them and the gold captive. She begged me to help her, but I being only one man could do nothing against so many. I was on my way to get help when the man that got away ambushed me last night. I escaped in the dark. You know the rest of the story."

LaRue studied the man for a moment. "Did you get a look at the man who shot you?"

"No, everything happened so fast, but I can tell you who it was!"

"If you didn't get a look at him, how can you know who it was?" LaRue inquired.

"Easy. He had a Sharps and there's only one man that uses one of them these days."

"Who might that be?" LaRue was finding this conversation very interesting.

"His name's Madigan!"

"Madigan, the army scout?" LaRue found it hard to believe that the man they called the man hunter would be any party to rape and murder.

"That's the one. You hear of him?"

"I've heard people talk of him. Don't know him myself, though. How can you be sure that it's really him? Just 'cause a man carries a Sharps doesn't mean he's this Madigan."

"Oh, it was him all right. I'd know him anywhere. You can take my word for it!"

How's that, if he didn't see him, LaRue wondered to himself. He was not about to take this stranger's word for anything right now.

"Eat up! There's more if you want it," LaRue said as he moved away from the man. O'Neill eyed him suspiciously.

LaRue found Shorty over by the horses. "Come with me, Shorty. I feel like a walk." Shorty put his plate of beans down and came up beside LaRue.

"What's up?" he asked the big man. "That stranger making you a little nervous too?"

"The stranger is a fake. You know it and I know it, but I'm afraid our men may think he's telling the truth. That might lead to problems for us."

"You think we should send him away? Might avoid trouble if we do."

LaRue thought for a minute. "It's not as easy as that. If we get rid of him now, the others will start asking questions, questions that could only lead to trouble. So you see, no matter what we do right now, we got trouble."

"I see what you mean. Can't do anything without stirring up a little manure. What do you suggest?"

"Don't rightly know. Just wait for him to make his move first, I guess. Keep an eye on him if you will. Maybe if he sees we're watching, he'll take it on his own to pack up and leave."

"Maybe we'll get lucky and he'll push me a little too hard. My friend here can end any trouble real quick." Shorty raised his Colt slowly out in front of him, then in a flash holstered it again.

"Let's hope we'll not need that," LaRue commented.

For the next two days, as LaRue's band traveled steadily westward, O'Neill gained followers. It wasn't hard to understand why. LaRue's group had been brought together for the purpose of finding the very gold that O'Neill now promised he could find. LaRue was losing his hold on his men again, and he knew this time he would not get it back, for the lust for gold was strong and these men LaRue had assembled for his expedition were an illiterate bunch at best. They lived for the moment and were ready to follow anyone able to lead them the sooner to riches. Shorty agreed with LaRue that a showdown was imminent.

On the third day it came. LaRue had been scouting ahead when he saw a rider coming. As the rider approached he saw that it was his friend Shorty and that he was in a hurry. A packhorse trailed behind him. LaRue put his rifle back in its scabbard and greeted the small gunman as he came closer.

"I'm up here, Shorty. What's with the packhorse?"

Shorty drew up abreast of Pete. "It's that O'Neill fellow. He's talked the rest of the men into setting an ambush for you when you come back to camp. With all the talk he's been doing about knowing where the gold is, the men agreed to follow him."

"Then why the ambush? If they all agreed by their own choice, there's nothing I can do about it."

"He says you're in cahoots with Madigan and that if they don't kill you first, you'll set a trap for them after they have the gold. You know there's not a smart one in that lot, so they believed him to the letter."

"How'd they plan to get me?"

Shorty smiled at his friend's question. "In the back, of course! Someone convinced O'Neill that you were too fast to take straight on, so he devised a plan to get your attention, then shoot you in the back while you were too helpless to do anything about it."

"They know we are friends. How'd you manage to get out with your body in one piece?"

"Real easy. At first they thought I was out of camp with you. When they realized I was back and had heard what they were planning, they offered to cut me in for a big share if I'd kill you."

"Why didn't you? May make you a rich man."

"Or a dead one! Just be a matter of time before someone took a rifle shot at me. From the rear, of course!"

"Why did they let you leave? You were outnumbered and they still let you go?"

Shorty grinned at his friend. "Anybody tell you that you ask a lot of questions?"

"You're the first. But how did you get away?"

"Simple. I told O'Neill if he gave me any trouble I'd kill him first, then kill as many others as I could before they got me."

"And O'Neill believed you?"

"Not at first, but the others made him believe it. None of them wanted to join him in the ground."

"So they just stood by while you packed up and left?"

"Not exactly. I made several of them pack up for me while I watched them and the rest of the bunch," he said with a grin. "Now I have a question for you. What the heck do we do now? O'Neill's got the men and most of the supplies. If he really does know where the gold is, which I doubt very much, he'll have it before we can do anything about it. We're only two against all of them. And here's another thing that's been on my mind: what do you think he'll do to any of those poor Indians that get in his way?"

"You mean Indian war parties?"

Shorty pulled his horse to a stop. "No, not war parties. I've heard rumors of a peaceful tribe of fair-skinned Indians that used to live in cliff dwellings. Then they moved one night to a valley that only they knew about. Maybe O'Neill found that valley. If he did, I wouldn't give a snowball's chance in hell for those people."

What Shorty was saying got LaRue to thinking. Could it be the last of the Aztecs that Shorty heard rumors about?

"One more thing," Shorty said, pausing. "You know I've never killed a man just to be killing, but in my book O'Neill needs killing and I'm thinking I'll be the one that does it!" With that, Shorty kicked his horse into action. LaRue moved his horse alongside his friend.

"It's not like you to hold a grudge. If you want to go back and kill O'Neill, I'd be the last to stand in your way. Just doesn't seem like you, that's all."

"I don't mean to go back after him. It's just that I have a feeling that he and I will meet again, and when we do, it will be him or me. Now let's put some ground between us before he sends someone out looking to cook our goose."

"You got a point there," LaRue agreed. The two men rode on in silence. There was nothing more to say.

CHAPTER 6

Behind a huge oak tree a few yards from the edge of the trail, the lean, dark figure of a man in war paint stood watching. Before him a lone rider on a magnificent buckskin was advancing slowly, a heavy-laden packhorse trailing along behind. The man rode along easily, almost nonchalantly. Yet the Indian knew that the rider would not be taken by surprise, for it was told in all their lodges of how this soldier fought bravely the Sioux, Shoshone, Ute, and sometimes the ruthless Apache.

This white warrior that sat his horse with the pride and confidence borne from many years and many battles would not be taken off guard. But the Indian had planned ahead. He was now joined by several other tribesmen who had come from an even larger group several hundred yards away. Then they waited for the enemy to get within striking distance.

Their plan was a simple one, to say the least. Since none of the Indians dared engage in hand-to-hand combat with this man, they planned to let him get within bow range and kill him by arrows shot from a number of directions.

Madigan's reputation was great amongst plains Indians, and even with these who lived and hunted the valleys between the mountains. Though it was considered a great honor to touch one's enemy while he was still alive and able to fight back, none of the Indians felt the urge to count coup on this great enemy before them.

The great buckskin had warned Madigan of the danger long before he sensed it himself. To turn back would almost certainly bring the Indians down around him in great numbers. To face a brave enemy was one thing, and Madigan knew, like wild animals sometimes afraid to attack head-on if their prey is strong, they would not hesitate to chase him if he ran. The scene was set and he could do nothing but play it through and hope for some break in his favor.

As they got closer to the Indians' hiding places, the big buckskin's ears perked up and he let out a blast of air through his wide-flared nostrils. His eyes darted from tree to tree, searching for the foul humans he smelled. These humans had the smell of fear, and the big horse wished to be given his rein so that he could carry his master fast and far from this place of fearful creatures wishing to do them harm.

Madigan and the horses were only a hundred feet away when the leader of the Indians started pulling back on his bow string. The long shaft of the arrow slid smoothly through his fingers as he drew it further back toward a spot on the right side of his chin. A few more feet and Madigan would be in the precise spot the Indians had picked for their attack. The brave glanced quickly around to make sure the others were also ready with their bows. He had carefully chosen each of them along with their hiding places to give the best possible chance of a clean kill on this enemy he was sure was about to die.

Where were the others? A moment before they had been within sight of him, yet out of sight of the enemy. Now they were nowhere to be seen, and the rider was just a few feet from the spot where they had planned to ambush him. He could not wait any longer. The Indian drew his arrow back the last few inches before he would let it fly toward its intended victim. There was no time to wonder or worry where the others were. A few more seconds and it would be too late. He must shoot now or the enemy might be lost. He would deal with the others later after he, Broken Bone, killed this mightiest of enemies by himself.

It was the Indian's guess that the others had run, being afraid of the power this man was supposed to possess. Broken Bone would show them, show them all, that his medicine was more powerful than that of this man. He carefully aimed for a point just below Madigan's neck, making sure to adjust his aim to allow for the movement of the horse and rider. Slowly the tension of his fingers relaxed and the arrow strained to be free.

The shaft of the arrow caught the sunlight as it flew silently through the air toward its target, flashing gold and silver as it arced downward on its flight of death. At first it seemed to go too high in the air, then at the last possible moment it dropped its nose and accelerated, only to end its errand by slamming into the Indian's body, pinning itself and the man to the big old oak tree.

At first there was no pain, just the sensation of pressure followed by a feeling of something warm running down the Indian's side from where the razor-sharp broad head had cut a wide channel through the man's flesh. His fingers released the final pressure from the rear of his own arrow letting it fly free from his bow. But it was no longer aimed on a path of destruction. For when the golden arrow had entered his side, it had taken most of the Indian's strength away. The bow in his hand dropped, allowing Broken Bone's arrow to bury itself harmlessly in the ground at the Indian's feet.

Broken Bone, now more dead than alive, watched as the bow fell from his hand, not understanding what had happened. This man Madigan was surely the most powerful of all men. For who but he can kill his enemies without raising a hand against them? Broken Bone's legs bent beneath him and he sagged against the tree, held there by the arrow with the silver-and-gold point.

As Madigan rode toward the suspected ambush sight, he casually reached down and slipped the thong from his Colt.

The buckskin pranced nervously under him, wanting to be done with this place. From under his hat brim Madigan surveyed the countryside on either side of the trail, looking for a hint of where the attack that he felt was imminent would take place. He was not a man to panic, yet he was no fool either. At this moment to be some other place was his greatest desire, but wishes have a habit of not coming true. So he rode on, ready to spring into action in a moment's notice.

The great horse under him, in his haste to be through this area of danger, kicked a small rock that went skittering off to the side of the trail. The sound it made was deafening to Madigan's ears and he was sure that at any moment Indians would appear from everywhere. He instinctively reached for his gun, but stopped himself before he had drawn it out of its holster.

Did the Indians see the move? Would it spook them into action? He held his breath and waited for a rush of bodies from everywhere. To his great surprise and relief, the attack never came. Was he imagining things, he wondered. Had he been on the trail too long? Madigan doubted it, for the buckskin had sensed peril also.

Something was there or had been, of that he was sure. But where had they gone, or were they waiting for a better chance somewhere up the path? He urged the horse into a gait, wanting to get out of this area as soon as possible. If by doing so he was hurrying into an ambush further ahead, he'd be ready. The prospect of a fight did not bother him as much as the unknowing.

The great horse again settled down to a slow walk, and Madigan relaxed. Whoever or whatever it was that had scared the buckskin was no longer a threat. He took off his hat and wiped the sweat from his brow. He was just putting the hat back on when he saw it, a flash of light maybe a mile in front and over to one side.

Playing a hunch, he quickly turned in time to see another flash of light back where he had first sensed trouble. Now

Madigan knew for sure what he had suspected for the last few days. He was being watched, but by whom he did not know. At any rate, they were taking a big risk following him through this hostile country. Could it be that the Indians he felt were there waiting in ambush had also seen the signals and decided to wait on those that were following?

Most of the flashes he had seen were ahead. It was only now that he had seen one behind him. It was as if they were waiting for him to come to them. For what reason, he did not know. But strange as it may sound, he did not fear them, whoever they were.

As he rode on thinking about the events of the day, he leaned to one side in the saddle to watch for tracks ahead. Puffs of dust were kicked up from the buckskin's hooves and they hung in the still mountain air as the great horse padded along.

There were no tracks to be found except from an occasional deer or elk. Then they crossed the print of a very large cougar and Madigan was glad that there was enough daylight left to be able to get miles from the big cat's territory before having to make camp for the night.

Had it been the smell of the cougar that had unnerved the buckskin? Maybe his discomfort at being close to the mountain lion had projected to Madigan. Yes, he reasoned, that was what had frightened them. The presence of a big cat is always reason to worry. Madigan laughed at himself. Must be old age creepin' in already, he thought. Couldn't have been Indians after all. A lone rider seemed like easy prey for them, and they had had the perfect opportunity to take his scalp any time in the last hour. He was sure it was the puma after all. But then again, there were the flashes of light behind him.

Madigan brought the buckskin to a halt and strained his ears to listen for any sound that might give away an attack in progress. Nothing. Only the chirp of a bird in the distance reached his ears. If there had been Indians, then whoever they were waiting for had eluded them. No, it must have been the cougar after all. He pulled his rifle out of its boot just in case he ran into the feline somewhere ahead.

A sharp tug on the packhorse's reins alerted him to trouble. Looking back he saw the pack animal regain its feet from a near fall. It had stumbled over some loose rock and was now limping. Just great, he thought. This whole trip had been nerve-racking. Now a lame pony with a big mountain lion close by and probably a hungry one at that, not to mention the distinct possibility of Indians. At least the Indians didn't eat you.

It wouldn't do to go any further. The packhorse's limp was getting worse and Madigan figured he had better find a place to camp for a few days and let the hoof heal. He scouted the surrounding countryside. There were a lot of fir trees in the area interspersed with stands of scrub oak. Every so often a small canyon would appear on either side of the trail.

If a man was careful he could camp up one of those canyons and have a good view of the trail below while keeping out of sight. Might even get lucky and find one with water in it. That'd make things a whole lot easier. If not, he had several large canteens in his pack and he could always sneak down to one of the many creeks and fill them up. Even with the horses drinking there'd be enough water for a full day, and hopefully the injury would be healed up in a day or two and they'd be back on their way again.

Madigan picked a place to his left where he saw a small tear in the rocks above that was only noticeable when he was directly across from it. If he had not been looking for just such a place, he'd have missed it altogether. A rock base led up to the opening that Madigan was sure the horses could manage if he was careful. So by continuing down the trail until it crossed a rocky stretch, then doubling back to the side of the trail a dozen yards, he'd leave no telltale tracks to give himself away. In the process of backtracking, he had the opportunity to fill his water canteens and did so. Madigan only hoped the rip in the rock led to a decent camping spot that might give him shelter from prying eyes.

It was more than he had hoped for. The narrow passage opened up into a small box canyon with a waterfall at one end. To the north was a stand of fir, and behind that was a flat area just large enough to conceal the camp from anyone who might venture into the canyon. If he used dry wood for the fire, he would not have to worry about any smoke giving him away. There was even a good patch of grass along the stream for the horses to graze on. After the last week, it looked like heaven to Madigan and he was quick to settle in.

After unloading the pack, he checked the packhorse's hoof. There on one side of the frog was a small cut that went unseen earlier when he examined the hoof for any injury. He took some water and washed it out, then took a small patch of tar that he carried for just such a purpose and put it in the sun on a rock to get hot and melt. He then unsaddled the buckskin and made camp. By this time the tar was good and hot. With a stick he placed some of this over the cut, smearing it around to make sure it covered the whole injury, then he cooled it with some water. Now nature would have to do its magic.

While riding in, Madigan had studied the canyon walls, which were steep and went up forever. About ten feet from the top were between fifty and seventy nesting pigeons. It couldn't be better. If anyone got above camp, the birds would warn him long before there was danger. The only place that really needed to be guarded was the entrance, and unless someone had seen him go in, there wasn't much chance of it being found by anyone riding by. And if someone did come through, the buckskin never seemed to sleep and would give the alarm.

Before long, Madigan felt fat and sassy. His belly was full of beans and side meat and he found a soft place to settle down for the night. He wondered how many canyons like this little paradise there were around here. No doubt the Indians have camped in many of them, but he found no sign of any such camps within these walls. He finished the piece of jerky he'd been chewing on for dessert, then spread the bedroll out in the soft, green grass. The horses grazed a few feet away. Madigan took one last look at the campfire to make sure it was out and closed his eyes for what he truly believed would be one of the best sleeps of his life. In a few minutes he was out to the world.

The nudge from the great buckskin awakened Madigan around two in the morning. He came awake instantly while reaching for his gun. Then he listened for all he was worth. At first he heard nothing. Then through the crisp mountain air he heard the faint sound of a baby crying.

Out here all alone a man's mind can do funny things to him, so Madigan made no judgments until he was sure of what he was hearing. Minutes seemed to go on for hours, then he heard the sound again only this time much closer. Although it sounded like a baby crying, Madigan recognized the sound of that made by a mountain lion, or puma, as they are called in the Southwest. From the pitch, Madigan knew it was a big cat. Probably the same lion whose tracks he'd seen earlier in the day.

The buckskin grew more restless but stood his ground; it looked as if the packhorse was about to run. Madigan got up and carefully caught her by the halter. Taking a short rope, he tied her to a stout tree where she would be out of danger and not get in his way if he had to get off a quick shot.

Madigan levered a round into his Winchester .44-40. There was little moonlight in the deep canyon so he knew he must find some way of spotting the cat if it came any closer. Finding his pack in the dark, he quickly pulled out a leather bag filled with black powder. When prospecting, one never knows when some powder will be needed to blast out an opening somewhere. So through habit he always kept some handy.

The mountain lion cried again, this time from just outside the entrance to Madigan's hiding place. Now he was sure it was on the scent of the horses and that the big cat was hungry. He also knew that where the horses' scent was strong, his would be too. Normally human scent stops a cat dead in its tracks. But if they are hurt or old and cannot hunt their normal prey, they turn to easier game. From its cry, he did not believe this cougar to be old.

Then a chilling thought struck him—rabies! He had seen many fox along the way, and wherever there was an abundance of fox, there was a high probability that there'd be some diseased animals close by. If a puma caught one of these sick animals, it would contract the sickness also.

A mountain lion with rabies feared nothing. And this cat was heading Madigan's way! Another thing that tended to confirm his theory was the fact that this cat was making more noise than normal for a cat on the prowl. Something was wrong and he'd better be prepared to defend himself and the livestock.

First thing he did was to get a fire going, which only took him a couple of minutes. The light from the fire was somewhat reassuring, but it only lit an area of about twenty feet. The lion could get within a few yards of him and he would not be able to see it. He waited for the cougar to scream again to make sure it was still outside the small canyon, then he stepped quickly into the darkness and paced off another twenty-five feet.

Scooping out a small depression in the dirt, he poured most of the black powder into it. Then he carefully poured a trail with the rest of the powder back to where he'd be waiting for the big cat. This took some time, as he had to be sure not to leave any breaks in the powder line. Now he nervously sat down with rifle in hand to wait.

It is a unique experience to sit out in the wilderness a hundred miles from help, in the dark, with a rabid mountain lion tracking you down. There isn't a gun made that looks big enough at these times. Madigan thought about getting the Sharps out, but if he missed the first shot, he would not have time for another.

Madigan's lever action Winchester in .44-40 caliber would do the job if his aim was good, as long as it didn't jam. In his haste to try for Harry O'Neill several days before, he'd inadvertently smashed the rifle into a tree in the dark. When he tried for one last shot at the bushwhacker as he was riding out, his rifle had jammed.

The next morning he cleaned it thoroughly and found that the bolt going through the cocking lever was bent. As long as he worked the lever slowly it worked all right, but if he got in a hurry it would jam. There was nothing he could do about it until he got to a town with a gunsmith. He made a mental note to work the lever as slowly as possible if a second shot was needed.

A series of short screams brought Madigan to full alert. Somewhere a short distance from him the big cougar was stalking his next meal—Madigan! The packhorse that he had wisely tied a short distance behind him was terrified. The buckskin was jittery but kept his ground. Madigan poked a stick in the fire behind him and strained to see into the darkness.

Even with all the noise the packhorse was making, he could hear the labored breathing of the puma in the darkness. He had not yet seen the glow from the cat's eyes, which meant it was keeping well out from the fire. Madigan's guess was that the cougar was just far enough along with rabies to slow it down some and cause it to lose its fear of man, but not far enough along to lose its natural fear of fire.

A few more hours and the cat might have just rushed in and attacked him without warning and that would have been that. Like he thought earlier, this whole trip had been very nerve-racking. He was thinking that he'd have been better off to have stayed with the army where he only had to fight Indians and Generals for a living.

The buckskin's ears pointed forward, looking off to Madigan's right where the fir trees were thickest. No wonder he was unable to see the feline's eyes. The big cat was using the trees as cover and was probably right now getting ready to make his charge. The hair on the back of Madigan's neck crawled as he grabbed a glowing stick from the fire and touched off the black powder. Even as the powder flared up, illuminating the area in a blinding flash, he only had time to see the mountain lion in full flight before it would be on him.

Madigan had no time to aim as he pulled the trigger, then dove for the ground, rolling in an effort to escape the cat's savage claws. He knew he had missed, but the cougar was blinded by the flash and it also missed. Madigan quickly came to his knees aligning the rifle in the direction of where the cat had landed. He jerked the Winchester's lever down to eject the spent shell and reload another.

To his shock, the lever came off in his hand! He dropped the rifle and grabbed for his Colt but found only an empty holster. His side arm had been thrown clear as he rolled to avoid the puma's attack. He retrieved the rifle and grasped it by the barrel to use as a club.

The cat was now in plain view from the light of the fire, saliva frothed from its mouth. It was crouched, ready to leap, when to Madigan's utter astonishment, the buckskin whirled around and with a bone-crushing kick, sent the mountain lion sailing through the air.

Madigan wasted no time in looking for his Colt. Finding it by the fire, he swooped it up and fired a quick shot in the direction of the cat in hopes of scaring it off. He spent the rest of the night watching and waiting for the cougar's return.

First light revealed one very large and very dead mountain lion fewer than twenty feet into the trees. The buckskin's kick had caved in its ribs and it had probably been dead before it hit the ground.

It took some time to bury the animal and it was hard work in this rocky soil, but he finished the job after about an hour.

"Don't want any more critters feeding off the carcass and getting sick too," he muttered to himself. One mad mountain lion was enough to last Madigan a lifetime!

The tar was helping to heal the packhorse's hoof and he figured in another day they'd be on their way again. And he could use some rest see'n how he didn't sleep much last night, but there was something that bothered him about being so close to that dead cougar, even though he had buried it deep. Never knew when its mate might come 'round, if it had a mate. The trouble was, if it did she'd sure as hell have the sickness too.

Madigan made plans just in case. First thing he did was to find some dry wood that would burn brightly. To this he added some dried branches covered with pitch from the fir trees. He made two piles of this dried wood, one at each side of camp. Now if any more trouble came his way, he could fire the wood and have plenty of light to see by for a good shot. Madigan was hoping he didn't have anything to worry about. With the stream running through the canyon, he had no worries about water and the grass was enough for the two horses for a week or more.

About noon the next day, he decided to take a look at the trail. Never hurt to do a little scouting when you were held up for a few days. The sun was high and the shadows were short; Madigan liked it that way. A short shadow was much harder to see and right now Madigan didn't want to be seen by anyone.

Just inside the entrance to the canyon there were some large boulders and past them a rock ledge went up the side of the cliff. Above the ledge there was an overhang, putting most of the ledge in shadow. Madigan took a good look around, then ascended to the ledge, keeping well back in the shadows so to be out of sight of anyone below.

Keeping a lookout for snakes, he was able to climb almost to the top of the cliff. By standing, he could just barely get a handhold and was able to pull himself over the top. From here it was a beautiful sight all around, and he lingered for a long while. No one was in sight below, so he moved back away from the edge and had a look at his surroundings.

From his high perch he was able to see down into the hideaway. There far below him, were the two horses grazing, and behind them the creek cascaded down the mountainside, ending in a crystal clear pool of blue-green water. Madigan was pleased to see that his campsite was not visible until he moved around to the other side of the canyon rim. As Madigan got close to the far rim, he was greeted with the frenzied flight of dozens of pigeons fluttering through the air in a madcap dash to be free from his intrusion. A better alarm he could not hope for.

It was getting hot, so Madigan made a quick check around and started back down. He had just dropped onto the ledge when he caught sight of movement far down the trail from which he had come the day before.

From his vantage point, he had a sweeping view of more than three miles on either side of him. Straining to see into the light, he made out two riders and a packhorse. They were in no hurry and as he watched, they would look over their shoulders from time to time. Looked like they figured to be followed. Why else would they be keeping such close track of their back trail, Madigan thought.

Madigan kept to the shadows and watched, not wanting to be seen coming down from the ledge. He only had his Colt with him; he had left the Sharps in camp, so if the riders saw him and were unfriendly, they had the advantage and could pick him off with their long guns. After finding a place to sit down out of the sun, Madigan settled in his lofty perch for however long it took for the riders to get out of sight.

Just up the trail from the opening to his canyon there was a small creek with a clear pool of cold mountain water. When the two men got to the stream they dismounted and started to make camp. This in itself didn't bother him, since they were far enough away so that the opening to Madigan's canyon was not visible to them. As long as they didn't get curious and start looking around, he had nothing to fear. Like most travelers in this country, they'd likely be on their way at first light.

Madigan waited for them to busy themselves before he slid to the base of the cliff and entered the canyon. The buckskin's ears perked up as Madigan approached. Only after recognizing his master did he start grazing again.

The moon was just coming over the rim of the canyon and the night chill was already in the air when Madigan rolled out his bedroll for the night. He was tired, more from the lack of doing anything all day than from anything else. He was about to take off his boots when the buckskin looked up toward the narrow canyon entrance and blew a rush of air from his nostrils. Madigan quickly changed his boots for the moccasins he always kept with him.

Something out there had caught the great horse's attention and he figured he'd better check it out. As he crept out into the open, the moonlight was casting eerie shadows around him and he had the feeling that he was no longer alone.

CHAPTER 7

Edging his way through the narrow corridor from his hideaway, Madigan crept silently toward some rocks that might shield him from searching eyes. In the moonlight he could see the long ribbon of trail below. To his left a small campfire was burning where the two men had camped. Although he could see it from his vantage point, he doubted whether anyone on the trail below could.

To the east a horse whinnied. Madigan peered into the direction of the sound. It took some time before his vision adjusted to the changing light. Milling around about a quarter mile away, he was just able to make out a party of riders. Even in the bright moonlight he was only able to see their movements. All else was lost at this range.

Before long a form broke off from the rest and moved slowly to the west. Waiting, Madigan was soon able to see the silhouette of a single rider as the man passed less than a hundred yards from him. It didn't take much to figure the drifter didn't want his presence known.

The absence of hoofbeats on the hard rock told him that the rider had tied pieces of leather or the like around his horse's hooves so they would make little noise as he rode along. It was a trick Madigan had used once to sneak away from some Indians that had it in mind to collect his scalp. Whoever the rider was, he hadn't been born yesterday. Watching him ride past, Madigan wondered what he was up to. Then he remembered the two men camped ahead.

It didn't take him long to realize the man had a mind of getting the drop on the camp in the dark, while the two men wouldn't be expecting trouble to come their way.

After the rider went by, Madigan followed on foot at a safe distance, so as not to make his presence known to the bushwhacker. A short distance from the camp, the rider dismounted and took a double-barreled shotgun from his saddle boot. Keeping to cover, he advanced on the camp carefully, the shotgun kept at the ready. Now it was plain to see what he was up to. This hombre had murder on his mind! And the two gents at camp were in for a nasty surprise.

Madigan closed in, keeping as much as he was able to the shadows. He was but five feet from the bushwhacker when the man unexpectedly turned around. Madigan froze, sure the man had seen him. For a long while they stood facing each other, sweat running off Madigan's forehead as though it were a hundred degrees in the shade. He didn't dare so much as breathe. Madigan swore he could see all the way down the shotgun's two barrels. All that was left was for the bushwhacker to pull the trigger. Madigan didn't have a hope in the world of beating him to the draw.

There in the moonlight the man's face was like a mask of doom. Every line, every pore, was clear to Madigan, from the man's narrow set eyes to his cruel mouth. Was this the face of death, Madigan wondered.

The dryness in his mouth was like a desert wind. But what was most startling was that he was not afraid. It was as if there were no longer any need to fear. Madigan was going to die and there was nothing more to be done. Fact was fact. The bushwhacker had him, nothing more, nothing less.

Madigan braced himself for the shock of the explosion. As he did, the man's cruel mouth slowly changed to a smile.

"Is that you, Ed?" the mouth whispered.

Not being one to pass up an opportunity to live, Madigan quickly replied in a whisper. "Yeah, it's me."

"Stay put while I blast these guys," the mouth returned.

"Right!"

The cutthroat lowered his gun, took a half-step around, then stopped. For a brief moment he seemed to be thinking. Without warning he swiveled around and came toward Madigan, the shotgun still lowered. A couple feet from Madigan, the killer looked like he was about to say something, but it was too late.

Madigan unleashed a right to the man's jaw that sent him to the ground. Another was not needed, for the man was knocked cold. Madigan kicked the shotgun away from the man, reached down, and took the man's handgun and knife. Why hadn't he realized Madigan wasn't his friend before he got so close? Turning, Madigan realized the full moon had been just over his shoulder. Its light was enough to make Madigan only a silhouette from where the man had been standing. Madigan once heard the saying that moonlight was for lovers—to him it was for life.

Now Madigan had another problem. The bushwhacker's friends were back there waiting for him to do his dastardly deed before they came in, and it was a sure thing Madigan didn't want to be here when they arrived. He not only had to be gone from this place himself, but he had to warn the two men in camp without giving himself away.

The man on the ground had planned to kill them as they slept by firing both barrels from the ten-gauge Greener into them at close range. The killer's friends down the trail were waiting to hear the blast before they continued on in, and even then they'd drift in slowly just in case things didn't go as planned. So far, nothing had disturbed the men in camp, but Madigan would change that shortly.

Taking up the shotgun, Madigan checked around to make sure of his exit, since finding a quick way out of here was essential to his survival. Satisfied with an escape route back to his camp that provided plenty of cover, he quickly walked back to the man on the ground. The killer was still unconscious, much to Madigan's satisfaction.

Yanking back the twin hammers on the scatter-gun, Madigan fired both barrels into the air. If that didn't wake somebody up they must already be dead, he thought. He had done all he was going to do to help the two strangers. They were now on their own, and Madigan hoped they could cut it.

Madigan dropped the ten-gauge, ran through the darkness, and didn't stop running until he was safely above the trail and at the opening to his hideaway.

At the blast and sudden flash of light from the shotgun, Shorty was up and running for cover, LaRue hot on his heels. The two men quickly took cover under the branches of a big old fir.

"What the hell was that?" asked LaRue.

Shorty was already checking his guns. "I don't know. You hurt anywhere?"

"Yeah, I think I've been wounded in the foot. It hurts something dreadful and I can feel blood. It must be pretty bad. It feels all mushy."

"Can't do much about it now. You think you can hold on for a little longer?" Shorty asked.

LaRue felt his foot again and grimaced. "I haven't got much choice, do I?"

Before them their empty camp shone in the light of their campfire, cooking utensils scattered about where the men had dropped them.

The men laid waiting for whatever was to come, but after several minutes no other sound was heard, and as far as they could tell, nothing moved.

"I'm going out there and see what's up. Better for me in the open facing someone than here where they can pick us off come daylight," Shorty said.

He charged off into the darkness, his passage marked only by an occasional twig breaking. LaRue tried to cover him but soon realized it was useless to even try. In the moonlight, there was no way of knowing who was who until it was too late.

Before long, LaRue was aware of someone coming toward him from around the other side of camp. All he could do was wait.

"Pete! It's me, Shorty," came the low voice through the night. In a short time Shorty was again at LaRue's side.

"Find anything out there?"

"Yeah, I found John over the other side of camp knocked out cold!"

"What was he doing over there?"

"Don't know; never asked him, but his ten-gauge had been fired. That's what we heard no doubt."

"Then O'Neill can't be far behind. Probably sent John ahead to finish us off while our backs were turned. How the hell did he get knocked out? Did he trip and fall you think?"

"Not hardly. I thought the same thing, but he's on his back and his mouth is torn up some. Besides, no rocks within ten feet of him and his side arms are gone."

"Might have got thrown from his horse and wandered in close to camp before passing out," LaRue offered.

"Maybe, but he wouldn't have been able to get his shotgun if he was thrown. More likely he was sneakin' up on us and somethin' or someone attacked him."

The two men looked at each other, both wondering the same thing. Who had put Smith down and then left in the night? LaRue was the first to voice his thoughts.

"You don't think Madigan is about, do you?"

Shorty nodded toward where John Smith lay. "I know it wasn't Indians who did it. John's still got his hair in one piece and his throat's not cut. Whoever it was no doubt saved our lives, and now I suggest we clear camp before the rest of the boys come moseying around. They sure as heck heard the shot and will be sneaking in any time now."

Pete agreed. It was a good idea to get out while the getting was good.

"Better kick some dirt on the fire. No use giving our location away if we don't have to. How's your foot doing?"

"Wasn't as bad as I thought," LaRue answered sheepishly. "In my hurry to take cover I must've burnt it when I stepped in the frying pan full of beans. That's the last time I take my boots off before it's time to turn in. You hungry? Still got some of those beans left."

Shorty wanted to laugh but didn't dare for fear of being heard.

By first light Shorty and LaRue had moved several miles down the trail and had their horses picketed in a high, hidden meadow overlooking their back trail.

"We better get some sleep while we can. I'll stand first watch," LaRue said. An hour later LaRue woke Shorty up from his nap.

"Look what's coming up the trail," LaRue said. He motioned to Shorty to keep hidden while he came to look. On the main trail O'Neill and his men were riding by. John Smith sat loose in his saddle rubbing his chin. The saddle boot where he kept his ten-gauge was empty. The shotgun now belonged to Shorty.

O'Neill wheeled his horse around and came up beside Smith. "You sure you don't know who hit you?" he asked, a look of disgust on his face. Smith looked down at his saddle horn, afraid to look O'Neill in the eye.

"Like I said, I thought it was Ed and a couple of the boys. They were standing in the shadows with the moon behind them. The next thing I know someone grabs me from behind and holds me while the other hit me with the butt of a rifle. That's all I remember until you found me. What more can I tell you? I didn't have a chance against three of them laying in wait for me like that. They just didn't play fair!"

"Three of them, huh? They're not as dumb as I took them

to be. Somehow they found themselves a friend," O'Neill said. "Course, if they were smart they would have killed you when they had you." And saved me the trouble later, O'Neill thought to himself.

Smith was glad when O'Neill rode on ahead, leaving him to nurse his chin. At the next town he figured to bug out and leave O'Neill and the others to whatever fate they had coming to them. After last night Smith just wasn't in the mood for this kind of life anymore.

Shorty grinned at the sight of the haggard band of outlaws moving by. "I don't know whether it's better to be behind them or in front, but we best keep our eyes peeled from here on.

"Any ideas on how we can beat this thing? I don't think O'Neill's the kind of man to let things lie. And there's the matter of whoever saved our bacon last night," Shorty said. "I don't suppose Smith will forget whoever it was that knocked him out either. He'll be wantin' another chance to even the score."

"Right now we got a friend out there, and I for one don't mean to make an enemy of him. If he was able to get Smith like he did, then there's nothing stopping him from getting us any time he wants. I think our best bet is to stay right here for a day and rest up. By that time O'Neill's bunch will more than likely move on and forget about us." LaRue pursed his lips in thought. "What about tracks? They'll be lookin' for 'em and when they don't find any, they'll know we gave them the slip. What then?" LaRue asked.

Shorty watched as the last rider rode out of view before speaking. "More 'n likely, he'll figure we went the other way. Not much chance of any of the men wanting to go back lookin' for us. Not with all that gold on their minds that O'Neill is suppose to know the whereabouts of."

"See what you mean," LaRue said. "Course, O'Neill won't want to chance us doggin' his back trail, so he'll likely set an ambush just in case."

Shorty smiled a rare smile. "That's why we wait around for another day. When we don't show in four or five hours, he'll be convinced we gave up and headed back East."

Madigan made his way back to his camp in the little canyon without incident. But before he called it a day he waited at the entrance until he heard the rest of the riders go by. Now that they had gone on, he had little fear his own camp would be disturbed in the night, and he hoped the two men below had used the chance he had provided to the best of their advantage. It had been close to half an hour before the others rode in, so they had more than enough time to clear camp and be on their way.

The buckskin grazed peacefully as Madigan pulled his blanket over himself for a much needed rest. When was he going to learn that one of these days doing good deeds like that was going to get him killed? Probably never, he thought.

The next morning he examined the packhorse's hoof and was relieved to see it was healing nicely. He'd give it one more day to make sure it was all right, then continue on his way. A cool breeze blew all day and Madigan spent the time fishing in the little creek in the canyon. It produced some fine rainbows, which he promptly ate.

After that he took a bath in the waterfall's chilling water, nearly freezing his rear off. His clothes also got a good cleaning, something they more than needed. Leaving them to dry, Madigan laid his blanket down in the shade and took some shut-eye.

The next morning dawned bright and clear and he was anxious to be on his way again. The crisp mountain air gave him an appetite for once, but before fixing breakfast he checked the packhorse's sore hoof by walking her around camp with a light load on. There was no sign of a limp, so he set his mind to hurry and eat so that he might make some distance before the heat of the day.

An hour later he was packed and started on his way. It

would be a long time before he found anything like this secluded shelter again, and there was a great hesitancy in his heart to leave this beautiful place that had hidden him so well from his enemies. But the time had come to push on, and though he did so unwillingly at first, he was soon lost in the excitement of the new sights and sounds of the ever-changing panorama before him.

Now, Madigan was a man of caution, and when he traveled, he kept out of view as much as possible. This habit of his had kept him away from trouble more than once.

He was doing just that—keeping from sight—when up ahead and to his right he glimpsed two riders and a pack animal advancing toward the main trail. They were coming down through the pucker brush from behind an outcropping of rock. The two were moving along easy like, not stirring up any dust, while keeping a close watch on the trail in front of them. Madigan figured it must be the two he'd saved a few nights before.

There was plenty of cover around, so he just let them ride on ahead while he held back for a spell. At least they had sense enough to get off the trail for a day and let trouble leave the area. Now he'd do the same, just drift along nice and slow while they rode on ahead and put some miles between him and them. Been so long since he'd really talked with anyone that wasn't trying to kill him that he was tempted to catch up and say howdy, but knew better.

Before long, he came to what looked like a game trail angling off to the north and up the side of the mountain. Madigan realized it might afford him a better look at what was up ahead while allowing him to stay hidden much of the time. He decided to follow it a ways; if nothing else it would help to put more miles between him and the two riders ahead. Dropping to the ground, he led the two horses along the narrow, twisting path between sparse stands of fir. Once he startled a big buck with a doe in tow and watched it go bounding off through the brush with a speed that never failed to amaze him.

After a short distance the path widened and he mounted up again. At times the going got rough, but the buckskin took it in stride, only stopping from time to time to wait for the packhorse to struggle over an obstacle that the buckskin was able to hurdle easily.

Before crossing a creek that flowed across his path, he allowed the animals to drink their fill of the sweet mountain water before mounting up again. Madigan thought that the trail would've allowed him a view of the lower ground before this, yet each time it looked as though it was about to come out on a vantage point, it turned away. At the very least, by doing so he was never in view of anyone below.

Realizing he'd have to go to the top before he'd have his look, he impatiently hurried the buckskin on with a slight kick to his ribs. Just a tap really, but the great horse got the picture and soon they were nearing the top of the trail where the ground flattened out into a kind of terrace that hung to the side of the mountain like some kind of perch for a giant bird.

Now, Madigan was no fool. So when he got within a hundred yards or so of the top, he picketed the horses and went the rest of the way on foot. If he figured the place for a good lookout, there was no reason someone else hadn't done the same.

He slipped the thong from his Colt just in case and walked wearily out of the brush onto the flat clearing. If a view was what he wanted, then that was exactly what he got. Only it wasn't of the valley floor below. Instead, as he stepped into the clearing, he was immediately confronted with the sight of twenty or more Utes with blood in their eyes. A chill ran down his spine. Madigan was trapped with no place to go! There wasn't one of them Indians that didn't have an arrow pointed right at him!

Behind him the buckskin snorted and shortly afterward Madigan heard a thud and figured the great horse had gotten himself a Ute that had approached too close. He only hoped they'd turn the horse loose and not kill him where he stood. It was a sure bet that he'd not be needing a horse any more. He felt a sharp prick in his back, then a hand lifted his gun from its holster. The same hand also found and took his knife. Now totally disarmed, Madigan felt his heart sink as never before.

He was taken to a large tree in the center of the opening where dry brush and dead wood were soon piled around the base, and Madigan didn't have to be told what they had in mind for him. At different times in his travels he'd come across burned-out trees in the middle of clearings such as this, and had wondered why a single tree was destroyed and not others around it, as would be the case in a forest fire. Madigan had thought of the possibility of lightning but the tree would not be blown apart like a lightning strike does.

Now he realized those trees had been used to burn the hated whites that had dared challenge the Indians and lost. Madigan envisioned someone years from now riding through and wondering about this tree. Would he know that a man had died while tied to it as it burned? Whether he did or not was no matter to him.

A sharp blow knocked him off his feet and for a moment bright lights danced in his head. He felt himself falling, then nothing.

Madigan didn't know how long he was out but it couldn't have been long. He'd been carried to the tree and was held to its trunk by a rawhide rope wrapped around it and himself. Only his hands were free, but he could do nothing with them to help himself.

Some of the Indians were dancing what he took to be some kind of a death dance, their painted bodies glistening in the sun. Others were using a fire bow, trying to get a fire going, and from time to time they'd look up at Madigan and laugh. The rest of the Indians just stood around or sat watching him with a look of amusement on their faces. To Madigan it was not amusing at all.

He questioned his hands being left untied, but the answer was soon coming when several Indians came toward him with another length of rope. As they came closer, one of them thrust the point of a lance under his chin—Madigan assumed it was to keep him from struggling—while they tied his hands behind him. The blade of the lance was held with such pressure that it cut flesh, and a small trickle of blood ran down his neck to be lost somewhere in his shirt.

Madigan struggled with the idea of forcing his body forward onto the razor-sharp blade of obsidian, thus ending his life quickly, giving the savages no satisfaction of their own. Yet something deep within him kept him from it.

Madigan stood there unmoving as a loop of rope was placed around his left hand and jerked tight pulling his arm up behind him. He felt his right arm being lifted so that it too could be tied. All at once an unnerving shriek filled the air. The tension on his left hand suddenly released, allowing it to drop to his side along with the short piece of rope attached to it.

Every Ute stopped what he was doing. They all gathered around the one Indian, who had just before been tying Madigan's hands behind him. The Indian kept jumping up and down pointing to Madigan's side where his right hand now hung. Several of the Indian's comrades came closer for a better look at what he was pointing to. They too were soon jumping and shouting and pointing. Finally the Indian, who Madigan took to be the leader, came over and grabbed his right hand.

Madigan watched him closely. The brave first looked at Madigan, then his eyes swept down to his hand, then back to his face. His cold, black eyes that a moment before had been filled with contempt now were filled with fear. Madigan was vaguely aware of the old Indian releasing his hand, and in a single move the brave and his band moved back into the brush that surrounded the opening.

In seconds they were gone. In his haste to be away, his guard had dropped the lance at Madigan's feet. Bending over, he got hold of it and used it to cut himself loose.

Was this some kind of a trick? He hoped not, for he was not in the mood for jokes at the moment. What had it been that had scared them so?

He started to rub his left wrist where the rope made it raw, and in doing so, saw the ring on his right hand, the silver and gold band the women had given him after he rescued them. Was this what had frightened his capturers away? Indians are a superstitious lot, and if it was the ring, then it must mean big medicine to them. Ring or not, Madigan was glad to be free and wasted no time getting his gun back from where it had been dropped by the edge of the clearing.

Being a man who always finished what he started, he walked briskly to a spot where he could see the ground below and to the west. There far ahead were the two riders; no one else was to be seen. Madigan was more than a little nervous about sticking around after his meeting with the Utes, so he wasted no time in getting back to where the horses were tied. A dead Ute lay to the rear of the buckskin and it was obvious the big stallion wanted to be rid of this place as fast as he could.

It took a lot less time to descend the side of the mountain than it took to come up. Once back on the main trail Madigan took out his rifle and made sure it was loaded. Funny, it hadn't felt so hot a few minutes ago!

CHAPTER 8

O'Neill was growing uneasy, and his temper was starting to show. He had been waiting hours for LaRue and Shorty to appear. The sun overhead was merciless in its dance across the sky, baking those below who watched for the victims they hoped to sacrifice in their quest for gold.

"Hell, they ain't coming!" Morales complained as he wiped his brow with a dirty sleeve. "They probably hightailed it back East where they'd be safe."

O'Neill thought over what Morales said for a moment before making a decision. It was hot out all right, and this place had no water close by. O'Neill deliberately picked this spot to bushwhack LaRue and his friend, knowing they would be in a hurry to get through this wasteland.

There was nothing here but rock and brush with a few burned out snags to testify to a fire that almost certainly had devoured most of the other trees. Without a sufficient supply of water, the trees were having a tough time growing back. The brush, needing less moisture, was thriving, thus making a large meadow of little else. Further to the west a small hill, more of a knob really, rose to a height of thirty feet. O'Neill had the horses hidden behind this. Then he ordered his men to go out in the brush and wait.

"How long's it been?" O'Neill asked no one in particular.

"From the look of the sun, I'd make it out somewhere close to five hours or so."

"Doesn't any of you fools have a watch, for crying out loud?" O'Neill asked in anger, the gash on the side of his face growing redder.

"Don't you have one?" a sharp voice came back.

"He's the boss! He doesn't need one!" another voice piped in sarcastically. O'Neill knew enough to shut up while he was still in control.

The men were hot and thirsty. They'd been hiding in the brush under the burning sun, and they'd be in no mood to take any guff from the likes of him. O'Neill let the insult go unanswered.

"Come on in!" O'Neill ordered. "I think maybe Morales is right. They've had enough and are heading back home with their tails tucked between their legs." O'Neill let out a reassuring laugh that sounded hollow and empty.

One by one from various areas of the bush, a man would rise from his hiding place, each with a look on his face that said O'Neill had kept them out too long. He'd have to think of something fast or the game might be lost. And these were the type of men that killed the losing captain.

"Men," he said when they were all back, "right now some of you aren't too happy with me for keeping you out there all these hours. I knew Shorty and LaRue weren't coming after the first hour . . ."

"What the hell!" one of the men broke in.

"Just let me finish!" O'Neill said harshly. "As I was saying, I knew they'd turned back after the first hour. But trapping them wasn't the only reason I sent you out there." The men looked around at one another, each wondering what O'Neill was up to.

"I sent you out in the blazing sun to test each and every one of you. I needed to know who I could count on and who I couldn't."

"Count on us for what?" a rough-looking cowboy asked. "How the hell can lying out in the heat let you know who you can count on and who you can't?"

The question came from John Smith, hoping to trip O'Neill up and make himself look better in the eyes of the men. O'Neill let the question ride.

"Before us is a future of riches, if we are lucky, and you men do as you're told. But one slip up, just one, and we might lose everything! I am glad to say that all of you passed the test and we are now ready to put my plan into action," he said. "Over the next week we will be covering as much ground as possible. It is important that we get to our destination at the time of, or just before, the next full moon. That gives us a little less than a month to get ready.

"If we are one day late, we will have to wait another month, a month that will give LaRue enough time to get more men together. I for one don't intend to fight him and the Injuns both. The Injuns will be bad enough. They've already been hit once and they won't be as easy the next time!" O'Neill looked around at the men. All eyes were on him. The lure of gold again captured their imaginations and they'd follow O'Neill to the very depths of hell to get their share if need be.

Since the attack on the mountain, Madigan hadn't seen hide nor hair of any living thing except an occasional ground squirrel scampering about in search of food or company. As he approached, they'd stand on their hind legs and let out a low whistling sound to warn of his presence.

From time to time, he'd pass the tracks of the riders ahead. To a scout as experienced as Madigan, it was evident a large body of horsemen had gone through the day before. There were also tracks of the two others just a few hours old.

Coming in sight of a low hill, he noticed the tracks of three horses leaving the trail. Madigan guessed the two riders became suspicious and decided to skirt the hill and a possible ambush. Riding on, it became all too clear that an ambush had indeed been planned. Had the two men been a day earlier or the killers waited a day longer, there would now be two corpses under dirt.

Madigan rode on and smiled to himself when the tracks of the two men came back on the trail. They had been caught off guard once and weren't going to let it happen again. Still, they were taking an awful big chance by riding the same trail at all. They must be in a big hurry for something, he mused.

Madigan rode into Durango at sunset. Durango was a town with a wild reputation of free-flowing whiskey, hard men, and soft-but-wild women. It was hot in the summer and cold as the icy fingers of hell in the winter, and many a cowpoke or hard rock miner out for a good time wound up on Durango's boot hill instead.

Rather than ride down Main Street, Madigan turned the buckskin down an alley and made his way around the back of the town. Coming to another alley, he glanced down it and saw the front of the local saloon, the Durango Pleasure Palace.

The sun was down and Madigan had little fear of being spotted in the darkness between the buildings, so he moved closer to Main Street for a better look while still remaining hidden from prying eyes from the saloon.

Beside the Pleasure Palace was a makeshift corral, while a loafing shed stood to one side. Inside the corral were six horses with various brands. Some of the brands he recognized as being from large Texas spreads known for their rough ways and tough men—men that didn't think twice about leaving with one of the ranch's cow ponies.

Madigan had no doubt that these were the horses of the hombres that had followed the two men several nights back. An uneasy feeling crept through Madigan as he realized the potential for disaster if he got careless for even a minute.

Madigan took a last look along the street while he patted the buckskin on the neck. "Hope there's more than one livery in town," he told the big horse, "or we might be in a little trouble."

Reining the big horse around, he started out of the alley

when a noise caught his attention; it came from somewhere above. He froze, a reaction borne of years as an army scout. Two stories above, a window was raised and he could hear voices and laughter coming from inside. Suddenly a basin of water was thrown out the open window, followed shortly by a woman's face peering down. The water spattered on the ground a few feet away from Madigan. The woman's face was quickly withdrawn and Madigan wondered why people threw things first, then looked to see if anyone was below.

Another sound caught his attention, and he looked up again just in time to see the face of a man retreat out of sight at the same window. He only got a look at it for an instant before the face vanished back into the room. But it was enough for him to know that it was the same man he had clobbered in the moonlight several nights back.

Not being able to see the front of the building, Madigan surmised it must be another saloon or cheap boardinghouse. Most men on the move didn't have much money to spend on room and board, and most of them liked to wash the trail dust out of their throats after a long ride, so there were always cheap rooms to be had close to one or more of the saloons in town. Sometimes the rooms were right in the saloon itself and many had girls available for the price of a few drinks. Madigan made a mental note to stay clear of this end of town.

Riding down the back street, his packhorse in tow, he soon came to the back side of a livery stable. There was a small corral in back and into this Madigan unsaddled and put the horses. He had just closed the gate when an old man with snowy white hair appeared from nowhere carrying a sawed-off twelve-gauge.

"Can I get them some corn, stranger?" he asked. The man had come on him like a cat stalks a mouse, taking Madigan totally unaware. In a flash too quick for the eye to follow, he palmed his Colt.

"No need for that, mister!" the old man said. "Wouldn't do you no good anyhow; you shoot me and Bertha here goes off and cuts you in two. And we'd both be sorrier for the experience! This here sawed-off's got the triggers tied back and only my thumb is keeping the hammer from fallin'! Why, if I was just to twitch a little she's bound to go off! Be too bad if you happened to be standing in front of her when she did," the old man grinned. "Now about that corn, do you want 'em to have some or not?"

"Sorry, old-timer. I'm just a little tired and edgy. Had me some trouble back up the trail a ways." Madigan dropped the Colt back into the holster. "Meant you no harm."

The old man took a long look, then spoke. "What kind of trouble you talking about? Now be sure of what you say, stranger. The information's for me and me alone."

Madigan wasn't in the habit of telling others his business or, for that matter, his problems. But there's something about looking down the twin barrels of a sawed-off twelve-gauge that loosens a man's tongue a mite, especially when the man holding that twelve-gauge looks to mean business.

So Madigan told him about the men chasing him after he was forced to kill one of them in self-defense and of having to knock another man out to keep him from bushwhacking two other men. All the while the old man kept the shotgun leveled at Madigan's midsection.

After Madigan was through, the old man shifted his weight to the other foot and said, "You say you shot a couple out of their saddles at near half a mile? Only one man I heard tell that could shoot like that, but never heard much about him being quick with a short gun. From what I just saw, you're one of the fastest men I've ever seen with a Colt and I've seen plenty in my time." The old man hesitated while he spit out a wad of chew, never taking his eyes off Madigan or letting the shotgun waver. "Ain't always owned this stable, you know. Used to be marshal up to the rim country of Montana and parts east."

Madigan took a long, slow breath. He had guessed right about this old man. He was more than capable of letting the hammer drop. Something Madigan had seen in the old man's eyes had warned him that even though the man was old, he was still somebody to be reckoned with. Madigan hoped he could keep the man on his side.

"Used to be fast with a side gun myself, but gotten too old now," the old man said. "Can't see worth a darn. Never figured to live this long, so now I've got to use this." He shook the shotgun just enough to make his point, but not enough to take it out of Madigan's belly.

Suddenly Madigan felt tired. "Old man, you going to shoot me or what? I've been in the saddle all day and I'd like to find an outhouse before I mess my jeans!" The old man laughed a little but never relaxed the shotgun.

"I might shoot you yet; depending on who you say you are." There was a question in what the man had just said and Madigan took no time in answering.

"I'm Sam Madigan," he replied. The old man stood firm.

"You can prove that?" he asked.

"I can. I've got my army papers in my pack."

"Never mind the pack. You could have a gun hid there. Show me your rifle, the one you did the long-range shooting with!"

"It's in my pack also, right at the top, covered with a leather sheath."

"Get it with your left hand, real slow. Remember, this here's got a tied-back trigger. It's a wonder she hasn't gone off before now with all the bull we've been spreading."

Madigan carefully untied the corner of the pack and lifted it with his left hand, going slowly as not to upset the old man. "It's right here in this cover," Madigan said as he slid the .50-90 from its hiding place.

"That's enough!" the old man said. "Only one man I heard of carries a Sharps with a black walnut stock and a silver butt plate." He lowered his shotgun, letting the hammers down slowly, then held out his hand to Madigan. "Welcome to town, Mr. Madigan."

"Call me Sam. What do I call you?"

"Most folks only call me to supper any more," the old man laughed. "But my name's Talley, Roy Talley. Late of this place, but in my younger days I ramrodded some pretty tough towns along the way as town marshal. Then old age came creepin' at my door, and, well, you know how people are. They think when you get a little older you can't hold your own any more." Talley looked down at the shotgun in his hands.

"Sometimes they just get smarter. I did up till a few years ago, then I started to forget things. Little things at first, things that didn't matter much, then bigger things that could get me or someone killed. So I came here, bought myself the livery, and settled in."

Madigan could see a sadness on Roy's face, so he said nothing, just waited for the old-timer to talk again.

"Some of those things I kept forgetting were things like loading my guns. Ever faced a man in a gunfight when your gun was empty?" the old lawman asked.

"No, can't say I have."

"Well, I did once. Only, I didn't know my gun was empty. Just cleaned it an hour before and had forgotten to reload it!" the old marshal said, shaking his head.

"What happened?" Madigan wanted to know.

"A coyote of a gunslinger called me out in the street. We faced off about a hundred feet away and he drew iron. I was pretty darn fast in those days and before he could clear leather I had my gun leveled on him.

"To this day I don't know why I didn't pull the trigger. Anyhow, he just froze and we faced each other for what must have been two minutes before he let his gun fall back in its holster, then he turned on his heel and walked to his horse and left. Something inside told me not to press the matter and I didn't. Later I discovered my gun was empty." Talley chuckled to himself. "I turned my badge in that night and rode away a big man in that town just as I had in countless others. Only this time it was for keeps.

"Been a good life, and even though Durango's a rough and tumble town, I've been at peace here. I only get my dander up when someone comes sneakin' round my place in the dark."

Madigan looked at the old marshal and deep down inside felt sorry for him. Many good men had been used up by the wild towns of the West, only to be cast aside when his usefulness ended. It wasn't like a banker that retired, a respected member of the town. When a town marshal got too old for the job, there was nothing left but to leave town so that the new man taking over didn't feel like his toes were being stepped on.

Some of them, like Talley, were lucky enough to have saved some money, not easy to do on a marshal's salary. They bought themselves a small ranch or farm and settled in to live a less trying life than they had been used to. Some liked it, some didn't.

Others, with no money and no place to go, simply rode out of town a few miles and put a gun to their head. In a way, they were striking back at the town that had deserted them, for there would be a funeral and the townspeople would know what they had done. To most it made no difference, but to a few it was enough of a shock that they started small retirement funds for future peace officers in their later years. In time things would change, but for now many a man who had given his best for years looked forward to old age with fear. Madigan was glad that Talley had been one of those with a future, for in him Madigan could see many aspects of himself.

"Well, I'll be darned!" Talley said, shaking his head. Madigan looked at the old marshal wondering what was next. "I did it again!" he said, showing Madigan the shotgun that was now open, exposing two empty barrels.

"I'd suggest you check it every so often just to be sure it's loaded," Madigan advised him. "Never know when you might need to pull the trigger and you'll want to hear more than just a click when you do." Roy Talley looked at Madigan with a twinkle in his eye.

"Try to remember that, but I'll not have to worry about much if that happens, at least not for long. Now, Mr. Madigan, what I really want to know is, should I give your horses some corn or not?"

"Give them grain," Madigan answered.

CHAPTER 9

Madigan watched as Talley led the horses into a well-cleaned stall out of sight of the casual passerby. He had no reservations about leaving the buckskin and packhorse with the old marshal. They would be well taken care of, no doubt, and he was glad to have the opportunity to meet this once-legendary lawman of a day that Madigan was sure was fast coming to a close.

Rights of citizens to carry a gun for their own protection had already been taken from them in some of the eastern cities like New York, although most men still carried them hidden under their coats.

And Madigan had to admit that the basis for the law wasn't altogether bad in some places—places where a strong lawman did a good job of protecting the townspeople. Trouble was, there just weren't many places where a few men could protect the whole. And Madigan, like many of his breed, feared that in the end it would be the law-abiding people who lost out to the politicians that would take all from them.

Disarming the population just made it easier for the crook to steal from, and murder, the honest men and women. Yet, deep down in his heart, he knew the day was coming where honest men and women carrying a side arm would be a thing of the past if something weren't done to prevent it. Madigan hoped it would not come within his lifetime.

113

"By the way," Madigan asked, "where did you learn that trick of tying the trigger back?"

"There was a time when I was young and ornery enough to bite a rattlesnake. Got somethin' in my head in those days, and a person would be hard put to change me from it.

"Some Texas drovers came to town at the end of a drive and got all liquored up. Most of the time the trail boss kept 'em out of trouble, but not this time. A real hard case outfit this bunch was.

"Couple of the boys got into it with one of the men from town. If I remember right, he was just crossin' the street when, for no other reason than pure meanness, one of these hombres started a fight with him. It came to fist and before you know it, the drover was down for the count and everything should have been over. 'Cept the drover and his friend didn't see it that way. They ambushed the townsman and shot him in the back. Good man he was, too. Had a wife and child and was respected."

The old lawman looked Madigan straight in the eye. "Now I'm no bleeding heart, but after I jailed these murderous cutthroats I started hearing talk of lynching my prisoners.

"Didn't give a damn about the jailbirds; it was the good townspeople I was worried about. Lynching's bad business. If they were to get caught and have to go before the wrong judge, they'd stand a chance of gettin' the noose themselves.

I decided to get the prisoners to the county seat for trial, but it was a full day's ride and there was only one of me to do the job. And to make matters worse, I knew that I stood a good chance of being met on the trail by some of their friends. And that's what happened a couple of hours out of town, but I was ready for them." The old man laughed like someone remembering something funny from the past.

"They rode out in front of us and blocked the trail and just waited for us to ride up to them. You should have seen their faces when they saw I'd tied the triggers down and only my thumb was holding both of the hammers back! I'd had the blacksmith bend both hammer spurs so they came together at full cock, so it was real easy to hold 'em back with one hand.

"At close range a sawed-off double-barrel makes a hell of a mess and these boys knew it. Didn't take 'em long to figure what would happen to their friends if I took a bullet. They just rode off sayin' they'd get 'em out of jail in the next town or somethin' to the like. Didn't though. They both swung the next day at noon, with nary a sight of the boys that were to save 'em."

"That's quite a story, old-timer, and I'd say you were known for that Greener like I'm known for my Sharps! And if I remember right, they called you 'Shotgun Talley' after that," Madigan said.

"You're right on that account."

"Where's the best place for a tired man to stay the night?" Madigan asked Roy when he came out from feeding the animals. He waited as Talley scratched his head, then took a bite from his plug of tobacco.

"There's always the Palace down the other end of town. It's got rotgut and women who'll spend the night with a lonely man for the price of a few drinks and a short meal. Course, you wouldn't get much rest and would probably have a fight on your hands before the night was over!"

"Why's that, Roy?" Madigan asked, already knowing the answer.

"Like I said before, there's five or six real bad looking boys staying down there. My years as a lawman taught me to tell the real bad ones, and they're about as mean as they come! Now, if you don't mind a short ride, there's Anny's Hotel about a mile down the road. She doesn't allow no booze or women, but the rooms are clean and the food's the best anywhere within two days' ride of here. Hell, within a week's ride to be sure! Got her an Injun girl that does some of the cookin', and I'm tellin' ya, man, it's the best I ever ate! Why, every time that girl's not working, I just about starve to death trying to eat my own grub," he said with a look of disgust. "I'll be heading that way in a few minutes, so you can ride with me. In the morning just tell Anny to hoist up the flag and I'll send old Errand Boy out to fetch you back here."

"I'm a pretty early riser, and I wouldn't want to disturb anyone to come and get me. I can just walk," Madigan said, but like most Western men of his time, he didn't really like the idea.

"Wouldn't hear of it, and neither would Errand Boy! No matter what time you want to come in, he'll be rarin' to go."

"Must be some kind of man to do that," Madigan remarked.

The old gentleman chuckled. "Ain't no man. He's a horse! Anny and I trained him to walk back and forth from the livery to her hotel. He knows that when he gets there he'll get a bait of corn for his trouble. Saves me from having to drop what I'm doing to ride over."

Madigan was curious about something, knowing the type of men that frequented the area, so he voiced his curiosity.

"Aren't you afraid someone will steal him some night?"

"Hell, no! It's been tried! The fellow who took him didn't know his way around these parts and that horse just kept edging his way back towards town, and came in from a different direction. That poor boy thought it was a different town altogether. Didn't think so when we threw 'em in jail. Yep! That horse really likes his corn!"

Remembering the face in the window, the thought of staying at Anny's seemed like a good idea. "How long before you'll be ready to go?"

"Just as soon as I feed and water the rest of the stock. I'd say not more than fifteen minutes at the most. You got time for a quick look around if you got the desire. I'll wait for you before I head out."

Madigan thanked Roy and stepped into the darkness of the alley. He wasn't about to walk out in the light from the windows until he was sure all was quiet. There was no way he could be sure that he hadn't been recognized by the man in the window when he looked out on Madigan from above.

All appeared peaceful on Main Street, yet he felt an uneasiness about him, such as when one is in the woods and has the feeling of being watched, yet has no foundation for feeling that way. It has been said that it is caused by some primeval sense that we all still carry within ourselves, a throwback to our beginnings when we were often the hunted and not the hunter.

Throwback or not, Madigan trusted his instincts, and on more than one occasion doing so had saved his life. And he had good reason to be cautious now with all the gunmen in town. Madigan knew Durango would be no different than other towns he had passed through on his way to this time and place, so it might be better to leave while he could, before any trouble came his way.

It was too late! If Madigan had not been keyed up as much as he was, he might have missed the sound altogether. The sound was that of someone running behind him in the darkness. Madigan's first thought was to step out onto Main Street where the light from the saloon would give away anyone following him. Then, as it had done countless times before, a flash of insight hit. Whoever was behind Madigan wanted him to do exactly that—move out into the light where he would make a clear target.

Madigan pulled himself close to the side of the building where he hoped his outline would not show. Slipping his Colt from its holster, Madigan waited. He didn't have to wait long before the footsteps in the dark came closer. And whoever it was had the advantage on him, as there was no light behind the man to show his outline. Yet from where Madigan stood, he was between the man and Main Street. Any sudden move Madigan made would be revealed to him immediately. There was nothing for Madigan to do but keep still and see how the cards played out.

The footsteps stopped some fifteen feet from him. Had the

man seen him? If he had, Madigan would have to act fast, for the advantage was still with the other man.

"What are you following me for?" Madigan asked while trying to judge the man's exact location in the dark. No answer came forth, but from the sound of the man's feet shifting around, he had not known where Madigan was until he spoke to him out of the darkness.

Then the answer to Madigan's question came. A stab of flame followed by another. Madigan felt the two bullets strike the building close to his face splintering wood into his eyes, but his own gun was already spitting lead back through the night at the attacker. He shot six inches high, first to the right, then to the left of where he saw the flash from the other gun. The man must have been left-handed, for it was Madigan's second shot that struck home, and he heard the man fall to the ground with a thud and little movement thereafter.

From his right he heard men yelling, then the swinging doors of the Pleasure Palace burst open and several tough-looking cowboys came running out. They appeared confused, probably trying to find where the shots had come from. Soon they were joined by three other men, and they all started toward the alley where Madigan was standing. They were still fifty yards away when Madigan slipped from the back of the alley and walked back to the livery stable.

"I told you there was trouble in town tonight! Did you get him?" Talley asked.

"What makes you think it was me who did the shooting, Roy?"

The old marshal spit some chew out before replying. "Cause I was on my way back to the other corral when I sees this fellow go into the alley behind you. I always go around back of the buildings so I won't have to go by the saloon. Never know when some drunk might get to shooting and a stray bullet get me when I'm on my way home!" Roy exclaimed.

"I may yet die of a bullet, but it won't be from the gun of a drunk if I can help it." He spit out another stain of tobacco. It caught the wind and splashed on Madigan's boots.

"Sorry about that," Roy said with a sheepish grin. "Now, like I was saying, this hombre follows you into the alley, but before he does, he pulls his gun out of its holster. Don't take no durn fool to know what he's up to.

"I ran for my shotgun and was just slipping into the alley when all hell broke loose. Seemed like a small army in there. Only took a moment to realize you didn't need my help, and if you did it was too late by then anyhow. And I didn't want to be around when the rest of them hombres came hunting trouble."

As they stood talking, Roy was facing the alley from which Madigan had just come. The barn door was open and Madigan's back was to it, shielding him from anyone in that direction. Roy was standing slightly out from the door and had a good view of the entrance to the alley.

"Speaking of hunting trouble, here it comes now. You better get into the barn before they get here," Roy ordered.

"I can handle my share of trouble, if that's what they want," Madigan replied.

"Just do an old man a favor and get out of sight! I'm getting too damned old to be patching holes in my barn roof. And sure enough, if more shooting starts there's bound to be one of them gunmen get hit right off. And while he's falling, shoot two, three holes in my roof, or maybe me. So if you don't mind, I'll handle this so no one gets hurt, 'specially me!"

Madigan liked this old man and decided to play it his way. So he moved into the shadows where he would be unseen but would still have a clear shot if need be when the group of men approached.

"Howdy, boys. What's on your mind this evening?" the old marshal asked calmly.

A heavy set, gruff-voiced man stepped forward to act as spokesman for the rest. "Our friend's been murdered and we're hunting the bastard that did it! You see anything back here, old man?"

Roy Talley should have been an actor, Madigan thought as he watched the old marshal facing the gunmen.

"Not a thing, 'cept Naci Yellow Hand. Don't recall hearing no shots though. Course, I'm getting a little old and my mind sometimes wanders."

"You say you saw a man named Yellow Hand. What kind've man would be called Yellow Hand?" the man demanded of Talley.

"Not a man, least not like you or me . . . ."

"Never mind, old man. Did he come out of the alley?"

"Yep," Roy said absentmindedly.

"Well, man, what way did he go?"

"Who?"

"Yellow Hand!"

Roy's eyes opened wide at the name. "Yellow Hand around here?" he said as he started for the barn.

"Old man, where ya goin' so fast?" the gruff voice asked. "We're not done with you yet!" the man shouted after Roy, a puzzled look on his face.

Roy turned back for an instant. "Got to lock up if that Apache is around. Never know where he might be hiding! Comes along from time to time to kill himself a white man, then disappears. Nobody can catch that one!" Talley said as he slammed the barn door shut behind him.

"An Apache!" someone in the group cried. "I'm not looking for no Apache. They can kill you without you ever seeing them. I'm getting back to the saloon!"

"Smith shouldn't have been out here at this time of night anyway. Got what he deserved," came another voice from the crowd. Soon all the men were headed back to the saloon, leaving Smith's body to grow cold in the alley.

"Thanks, Roy," Madigan said as they were again left by themselves, "but why the story about the Apache? It was self-defense and I could have handled the likes of them."

Roy Talley took one last look through a crack in the door to make sure no one else was around. "If I hadn't made up that fool story, then seems to me they wouldn't be back at the saloon getting good and drunk. They would be right here trying to get someone else killed. And like I said, I don't want to be the one to catch a stray bullet! Now, how's about you and me getting ourselves a bite of the best chow around these parts?"

"Sounds good to me," Madigan agreed as he climbed up on the springboard for the ride out to Anny's.

Anny's boarding house was a two-story affair painted white with red shutters. A fence kept the livestock a short distance from the house while a swinging gate allowed the guests access to the walkway leading up to the large sun porch. Madigan immediately liked what he saw and looked forward to a hot meal and warm bed. And from the looks of this place, he was going to get both.

A sign out front declared: "No booze, women of the night, or drunkards allowed. All rules enforced with shotgun."

"This Anny mean what she says on that sign?" Madigan asked Roy as they pulled up to the hitching post.

"Every word of it," Roy replied with a twinkle in his eye.

The inside of the house was as clean as any place Madigan had ever laid eyes on. The meal was plentiful, the room as clean as his mother used to keep, and the other people dining there were pleasant, except for the long-haired preacher that kept eyeing Madigan's guns while commenting on the sins of the likes of men such as him. But Madigan never gave him much mind.

Men like that were usually cowards hiding behind the Good Book like a shield. When he finally tired of the man's banter, he gave him a hard look that must have frozen the poor man's tongue, for Madigan heard nothing more from him the remainder of the night. At least the man had the common sense to recognize a warning when he saw one.

Now, this is the way to live, Madigan thought to himself as

he drifted off to sleep. That night Madigan slept like a baby, feeling really safe for the first time in weeks.

The next morning, he was up at the crack of dawn and ready to be on his way. Coming down the stairs from his room, Madigan was surprised to smell bacon already cooking. Normally he'd skip breakfast, but the smell of that bacon made him decide to start out on a full stomach.

He had just sat down in the dining room when Anny appeared with a plate of food that could have fed two men.

"Figured you to be an early riser," she said as she set the plate in front of him.

"I'm not the only one, it seems," he said as he lifted a hot cup of coffee to his lips. Anny gave him a big smile that showed sparkling white teeth, a rarity for a woman Anny's age.

"I always liked a man that got the day started with the sun and a full stomach. Why, if I was twenty years younger I'd . . ."

"I'd be ten years old," Madigan cut in.

"Right!" Anny sighed as she dropped her arms to her sides. "Always too young!" she said with a laugh that seemed to light up the room. "Always too young."

True to Roy's word, as Madigan walked outside, there on the flagpole was a white piece of cloth. At the pole's base was a bait of corn. Madigan didn't have to look to know that a short distance away was a saddled horse galloping towards him. Errand Boy wanted his breakfast.

Madigan let the horse eat, then mounted up and was soon at the back of Roy's livery stable. The first rays of light threw long shadows on the ground and Madigan instinctively studied them for any sign of something out of place before dismounting. Roy was sitting on a bale of hay fiddling with an old harness. He looked up as Madigan approached.

"How'd you like your breakfast?" he asked.

"How'd you know I had some?" Madigan quipped.

Roy looked up at him and yawned. "Anny was fixin' yours

while I was finishing mine. What did you think—an old man like me just naturally gonna sleep all day? I been up so long I was just thinkin' about taking myself a well-earned nap," Roy said with another yawn. "By the way, seen something that might interest you."

"Some of them boys up and moving already?" Madigan asked with interest, knowing that if they were up and about, he was sure to have trouble before he could be rid of this town.

"Not any of them boys. They all got them some lady friends, so they'll be sleeping late. That you can be sure of. But last night when I got back, I see where they were joined by five more men. Must have wired some of their friends in the next town to join them," Roy said. "Anyway, getting back to what I was to say, about an hour ago I was just returning from Anny's when I saw a couple of strange-looking gents come riding up here to the back door of my stable."

"In what way were they strange?"

"Well, first off, one of them was a might taller than anyone I've ever seen in my life. Going close to six-feet-six, I'd wager." Roy shifted his weight on the bale of hay before going on with the rest of the story. "Now, if he was in the middle of a passel of tall men, he wouldn't have stood out so much. But the gent with him wasn't much bigger than a boy," Roy said seriously, while gesturing with his hand to show the height of the man.

"Sure it wasn't a man and his son you saw, old-timer?"

Roy winced at the name 'old-timer'. "No, the short gent was a grown man, I tell you. But one thing for sure, the guns he was a carrying weren't anything but full-grown Colts." Roy came to his feet and closed the gap between them to just a few feet. "Mr. Madigan, I got the funniest feelin' that man-boy can use those shootin' irons too! Just the way he handled himself, no show-off like a lot of the runts you see nowadays."

"You think he's a gun out for hire? A lot of them seem to be popping up on the trail heading for California."

"Oh, he's a gun hand all right, but I don't think you could

hire him with a wagon load of money. I've seen the likes of him once or twice in my day. No, he's got something more important on his mind, and his kind always get it done, or die trying."

Roy turned to walk away, stood, turned back around and scratched his chin, then said with a puzzled look on his face, "The short one took a good hard look around when he first rode up, then pulled a small book out of his saddlebag and wrote something in it! Damned if I'm not tellin' the truth!"

What Roy told Madigan about this little man had him curious, to say the least. A gunman that wrote things in a little book was as uncommon as an honest whore. But Madigan had no doubt that Roy said it just as it happened. Stranger things had taken place in the West. That he could attest to.

"What was the other one like?" he asked, his curiosity fully aroused by this time.

"Big. Big and kind've quiet. Had the look of an intelligent man, though. Wore his gun down low. As soon as he stepped down from his horse, he tied his holster down. I think he was prepared for any trouble that came his way."

"Did they give you an idea of what they wanted?"

"More'n that. They told me what they was doing in town. Said they needed supplies and didn't want to wait around for the general store to open. I told them Sherm Basketskill always opened early, so if they'd just go over, he was probably opened already."

"Did they?" Madigan asked.

"Did they what?"

"Did they go get what they needed?"

Roy spit another stain of chew, this time narrowly missing Madigan's boots. "Thought I was going to get you again, did-n't you?" he chuckled.

"Sure did," Madigan said, still waiting for an answer to his question.

"Oh, yeah. You was askin' about them two fellows. They did and they didn't. They got their supplies, but they paid me to go get them for 'em." Reaching into his pocket, Roy produced a shiny five-dollar gold piece. "Easiest money I ever came by in my life," he bragged. "Got the usual grub and some more ammunition. They both shoot .44-40's. Had me give their animals some grain and took a sack of corn with them to feed their horses on the trail. That's about all. In less than an hour they were here and gone again."

It didn't take Madigan long to figure that these were the same men that he had saved back on the trail. When you have done as much scouting as he had, you read the trail like some men read a book, and Madigan had often seen the small boot tracks in the dirt where they had stopped to rest their horses.

He had also been aware of the much bigger prints that were deeper than most he'd seen. It wasn't that the man had any bigger feet than other big men, it was how they pressed down in the soil when he walked, with even pressure on the sole, meaning that he was not bowlegged like many of the cowhands. Also, the toes always pointed straight ahead when he walked, much like an Indian.

Roy had mentioned one other thing. When the man spoke to his friend, he had a very slight accent. Roy took it to be French like he had heard once down in New Orleans. At any rate, these two were a curious mixture, of what Madigan did not know, but something told Madigan he would soon find out.

CHAPTER 10

Sam Madigan thought over the situation for a few minutes before making up his mind on what to do next.

"How'd you like to make another five-dollar gold piece?" he asked Roy.

"Who do I have to kill?" Roy asked with a grin, his lined face lighting up at the prospect of another five dollars.

"No one. Just get back to the store and pick up the things I have on this list."

Roy gave Madigan a curious look as he handed him the paper. "Boy, this must be my day," he said. "But you don't have to pay me. I'd gladly do it for you."

"Thanks anyway, Roy, but let me give you the money. You'll be taking a chance with all the cutthroats in town. If they see you, they're sure to ask questions. And that could mean trouble for you."

"Don't worry about me being seen," Talley said. "I'll go in the back door. Besides, those boys aren't about to get out of the sack before noon."

"By the way, does he stock much ammunition?" Madigan asked, remembering he was running low.

"Yep, in fact he might even have some for that big gun of yours."

"Get me a couple of boxes of .44-40's, and if he does have any of the big stuff, get me all he has of the .50-90's. It's getting hard to come by, so I always try to stock up when I can,"

Madigan explained. He handed Roy a twenty-dollar gold piece. "That ought to just about do it," he stated.

"I'm thinkin' more than enough," Talley said. Madigan watched as Roy pocketed the money and was soon out of sight as he turned the corner of a building at the far end of town.

Madigan took another look around him, then got busy getting the horses ready to leave as soon as Roy got back with his supplies.

From the balcony of the Pleasure Palace, a man stood smoking a long, foul-smelling cigar. The smoke rose up and drifted lazily around his face in the still morning air. From time to time the man would fan the smoke away from his eyes, then take another long pull on the stogie as he looked slowly down Main Street, first one way then the other.

He was about to go back inside to the warm bed where his woman for the night waited, when he noticed movement far down the road. It was early and the morning sun was still low in the east, throwing long shadows between the buildings on Main Street. Whatever it had been was now hidden in one of those shadows.

The man waited and was rewarded with the sight of an old man scurrying across the street to disappear along the far side of the store. As the man watched, the scar on the side of his face began to grow red in the morning light. Why would the old man be in such a hurry to cross the street, O'Neill wondered to himself. There is more to this than meets the eye he thought, and it might be wise to check it out.

"Honey, come back to bed," came a voice from behind him. For a moment the temptation was almost too great, but O'Neill fought back the desire and hurriedly pulled on his boots.

Descending the stairs two at a time, he was quickly out the door, and a short time later he found himself at the back door of the store. Carefully, he peered around the corner of the open door. There within was the old man talking to a younger man who O'Neill took to be the storekeeper. They were not expecting company, so they talked freely.

"Sherm," the old man was saying, "I need this list of goods filled as quickly as you can. You still got that ammunition for those buffalo guns?"

"Sure do. Can't get rid of it. What you want with that stuff?" the younger man queried. "The only time I ever sell that ammo is to the few mountain men that come through on a grizzly hunt now and again."

"Got a friend that wanted me to get some for him, but keep it to yourself for awhile will you, Sherm?"

"Anything you say, Roy. How much does he want? I have several different calibers. Which does he use?"

"Fifty-ninety's . He'll take all you got."

"That will be three boxes, then. That's the most I've sold of this stuff at one time since I opened this here place up! What's he use it for?"

"For shootin' things with."

"Hell, I know that, Roy, but why three boxes? Take a hell of a man to go through one box in a year, less'n he's wearing one of those old buffalo robes to protect his shoulder. Ever fire one of these things off, Roy?" Sherm asked, holding up a huge .50-90 cartridge.

"Not without a gun," Roy smarted back.

"You know what I mean! You ever shoot a Sharps .50-90?"

"Yeah, once, and that was enough. My shoulder was black and blue for a month of Sundays. But this boy does all right with it, you can bet your bottom dollar on that."

Sherm studied Roy for a moment before speaking. "Only one man I ever heard could shoot a .50-90 like you and me shoot a .44-40."

"And who might that be, Sherm?"

"A man by the name of Sam Madigan. But I hear tell he's over the other side of the Divide."

"Not any more he's not! He's over at my place right now fixin' to go on to California. Now hurry it up, Sherm. Those rascals at the Palace will be up before you get this stuff together."

So Madigan followed me, O'Neill cursed under his breath. And he's in town right now! As O'Neill listened to the two men inside, his first thought was to go over to the livery and shoot Madigan in the back. But being the coward that he was, he thought better of the idea. The only other option to him was to get a couple of men together and bushwhack Madigan when he came out of the stable.

O'Neill pondered the second idea for a brief minute before deciding against it, his reason being that it would show his men just how much of a yellow belly he was. No, he would have to figure another way to get this man that scarred him for life.

Somehow, somewhere, he would find a way to kill this man that he hated—not only for bringing him to trial and for the terrible wound he had inflicted on him, but for being the kind of man that everyone respected and looked up to, the kind of man that O'Neill knew he could never be. Yes, somewhere up the trail he would kill Madigan, but on his terms and in his way.

Roy was putting some of the supplies in a canvas bag when he stopped and tilted his head back. "Sherm, you been smoking those cheap cigars again?"

Sherm gave Roy a startled look. "You know I don't smoke."

"Yeah, I just remembered. So where's that smell coming from?"

Sherm sniffed at the air. "I smell something, but it's not anything I'd sell." He sniffed the air again, then walked to the back door of his shop. "Smells like someone lit up a cow pie," he remarked as he looked out the door.

"Anybody out there?" Roy asked.

"Don't see anyone, but there's a cigar butt still burning on the ground. Whoever threw it here is long gone now. Hope I didn't get anybody in trouble with all my fool questions."

"Too late to worry about it now. I'd better get over to the

stable and warn Madigan. Bring the rest of the stuff over when you get it together," Roy ordered as he hurried out the door and around the corner.

Madigan listened patiently as Roy ran down the events of the last few minutes. So, the very thing that he hoped to avoid was now upon him. With luck it might have been just the town gossip looking for news, but down in his gut he knew better. It would be a race with time now.

He planned on leaving as soon as the supplies arrived, but not without some reluctance. He had met a friend here, one of his own kind, and they were far and few between, so it was like leaving part of his family. Roy was sad at Madigan's leaving, too. He could see it in his eyes and hear it on the edge of his voice, but to stay would only bring more trouble Roy's way—and Madigan's also. Trouble that was better left far behind, and that's what he fully intended to do.

A few minutes later, Sherm showed up with the rest of the supplies. Madigan quickly loaded them on the packhorse, said his good-bye to Roy, and was on his way. Madigan couldn't help feeling that Roy wished he were riding along with him. But age has a way of keeping the body from doing the things the mind still believes it's capable of doing. So it was with Roy Talley; the mind was willing, but the body was not.

The trail turned southwest just out of town, and Madigan rode steadily onward for the first few miles, then turned his horses off the path to wait and see if he was being followed. Satisfied that he was alone, he started to remount when a curious thing caught his attention. There in the dirt were the large and small prints that he had seen before. So the two men he had saved were still ahead of him. And from the looks of the tracks, they weren't taking any chances either!

Now, Madigan had what could turn out to be a serious problem. Behind him were the cutthroats from town, ahead were the two men he had saved days before. Both parties would sooner or later be closing in on each other, with

Madigan in the middle. So Madigan would have to make a decision soon, whether to ride this trail or turn northward and take the longer trail to California.

Sometimes a man is compelled to do what he knows is not in the best interest of survival, spurred on by a longing inside to go just a little further, and so it was with Madigan. He continued to ride on toward the southwest and his destiny.

He was riding into the land of the Navajo and Hopi, and from what he had heard, they were at peace now, if Indians ever were at peace with the white man. But where there were Indians there could be trouble, and a lone rider had all the odds stacked against him from the start. Madigan checked his guns before riding on, wondering what the next few days would bring.

The Navajo was kin to the Apache, one of the most fearsome warrior tribes known to man, and they had long used the white man coming through their land as their own personal trading post. Only what they were trading left no white man alive.

In a few days Madigan would cut the northwestern corner of New Mexico, and a few days later, if he kept at it steady, would be in Arizona. The scenery was already changing as he rode further south. There were fewer trees and more canyons and cactus.

Sometimes the trail was hard to follow and he would have to dismount to check for tracks. And always there were the hoofprints of the two men's horses leading on as if they had been here countless times before and were following some unseen map in their minds.

On the second day, Madigan knew he had crossed into New Mexico, as ahead was a mountain he knew to be Shiprock Peak. Here the trail turned even more southward, and as Madigan rode deeper into the Navajo nation, he kept a weary eye out for any sign of trouble ahead.

At night he made a cold camp in whatever cover he could find, always checking for snakes among the rocks before settling down for the night. No man wants to wake and find a rattler in his bedroll with him, least of all Madigan.

Here the stars were the brightest he could ever remember

seeing, and they seemed to go on forever. And even though he was vigilant to danger, he could not recall sleeping on the trail as sound as he did these nights.

The next morning, he passed an old Navajo village whose people had disappeared years before. It gave him an eerie feeling as he skirted around it.

The trail was well marked by the two men ahead, and he had no trouble following it, only occasionally having to look where they had gone off the path to rest their horses. From time to time he would pass patches of quicksand and would have to detour around them to keep from being swallowed up.

On the third day out from Durango, Madigan topped a rise and saw dust rising miles behind him and knew that the rogues from town were unknowingly closing in on him. Judging from their position, he figured he still had a day before he had to take evasive action.

It was near noon when he stopped to get a bite to eat and contemplate his next move. The day was hotter than Madigan liked it, and the temptation to find a cool spot and take a nap was almost overpowering, but he resisted.

Letting his thoughts wander, Madigan soon realized he was irritated at having circumstances control his life, instead of him controlling his own fate. What started as a fairly simple trip to California had turned out to be a fight for his life.

There had been many times when he would have liked to fish a stream along the way or rest a day or two, taking in the beauty of his surroundings, but instead he had to be constantly on the alert for trouble.

He even entertained the thought of setting up an ambush for his followers. He could simply lead them into a deep canyon with shear walls on either side and pick them off one by one with the Sharps.

Out here no one would ever know, or care, for that matter. They would just be a pile of bones after the vultures got through with them, a pile of bones to ride on by and be glad they weren't your own.

The more Madigan thought about it, the more it sounded like just plain murder to him. He may have been a lot of things in his life, but a murderer was not one of them, so he solemnly rode on.

For the last few days there had been fewer trees and more barren ground. Sometimes he would ride through canyons with slick red rock walls going up three hundred feet or more, and the color was such that it made the rest of the landscape seem dull by comparison.

Madigan's guess was that he was riding into the Canyon De Chelly area, from the description Talley had given him. To his right were the Chuska Mountains and ahead the trail disappeared into a labyrinth of steep rock walls.

A chill was in the air and he stopped to put on a jacket while he checked his back trail. He had been riding up an incline for several miles and now was somewhat higher than the terrain behind him. From here he had a clear view for about twenty miles on his back trail.

And there in the distance, as he had expected, was the telltale dust cloud marking the progress of his enemies. He stood watching for a long while when something caught his attention only a few miles away. He stared hard but could no longer see anything. Was it his imagination or did he really see a wisp of smoke floating just above the rim rock?

After watching the spot for close to five minutes, he was convinced it was only the heat playing tricks on him in the late afternoon sun. Still, something told him he had better be careful.

CHAPTER 11

O'Neill couldn't believe his luck. He and James Thomas had ridden out hours ahead of the rest of the gang. The trail was dusty and little wind stirred to move the dust away. They were in broken country, the trees slowly dying away, leaving little else but rock and red-walled canyons. A thundercloud loomed over the mountains a few miles to the west, threatening rain and the possibility of flash floods.

Thomas, who rode slightly behind O'Neill, marveled at the rich color displayed around him, while O'Neill hardly seemed to notice or care. He was like a man possessed with one purpose, one reason for living—to find the treasure. But even more than that, he was obsessed with the idea of killing the man called Madigan.

The day was hot, and from time to time O'Neill's temper flared, leaving Thomas to wonder why he had volunteered to come along. For two days they had ridden hard, only taking time to rest the horses and leave trail markers at crucial points along the way for the others to follow.

Every so often the two men would climb high on the rocks above to look over the trail ahead. This time it unexpectedly paid off. There on the trail below, resting his horses, was the man O'Neill hated most in the world—Sam Madigan, the man O'Neill had sworn a vengeance to kill.

"Give me your rifle," O'Neill demanded of Thomas in a gruff voice, already reaching a dirty hand for the rifle the other man held. O'Neill had been too lazy to carry his own.

Thomas hesitated before giving it up. Did O'Neill see something on the trail below or was it just a ploy to disarm him, Thomas wondered. He thought about the events of the last few days and grew uneasy inside.

As the two men rode westward, Thomas would catch O'Neill mumbling to himself. It was hard to make out what he was saying, but Thomas was able to piece together enough to know O'Neill didn't want to share the gold with anyone more than he had to.

At times O'Neill would stare at Thomas with a cruel smile on his face, then quickly turn away saying nothing. It gave Thomas the creeps. Now O'Neill had his rifle.

"What's down there?" Thomas asked, expecting trouble from the man before him.

"Madigan! Sam Madigan! I'm going to kill that bastard before he can get away again," O'Neill growled, levering a round into the Winchester.

This was the perfect opportunity O'Neill had been waiting for. Dropping flat to the ground, he crawled slowly to the edge of the cliff, careful not to stir up any dust and give himself away to the man he was about to kill.

It could not have been better. From his position high on the rocks above, O'Neill had a clear shot. The sun was high and slightly over his back and anyone looking in his direction would be blinded by the light.

Ever so cautiously, he slid the barrel of the rifle into position, and braced it against the broken remains of a tree that had long since perished.

O'Neill's breathing was hard and fast. He deliberately drew in a long breath and let it out slowly, then another several times more before being satisfied that he was calm enough to make the kill.

Carefully lining the sights on his target below and taking one last breath, he squeezed the trigger. The rifle jumped in his hands, the explosion deafening to his ears, the blast momentarily obscuring his view of the man below. When the smoke cleared enough to see, he was rewarded with the sight of his most hated enemy laying on his back in the dirt below.

"I hit the bastard!" O'Neill yelled, excitedly throwing the rifle back to Thomas. "Let's get down there and finish him off."

It was a long and dangerous climb down to their horses over loose and crumbling rock with little, if any, handholds to steady themselves by. It had been much easier going up, and O'Neill cursed the distance as he wiped the sweat from his brow. Once in his haste, he slipped toward the edge of the cliff but caught himself just in time. Only his hat suffered the fall and O'Neill cursed again. Finally they were down.

Riding cautiously, they approached the spot where Madigan lay, their guns at the ready. "Damn, he's gone!" yelled O'Neill as he suddenly turned his horse and rode for cover, not wanting to be the victim of his own trap. Spinning his horse around a large boulder, O'Neill quickly dismounted and threw himself up against the side of the huge rock.

Nothing stirred except Thomas running up beside him.

"Where the hell is he?" Thomas demanded.

"Your guess is as good as mine. One thing's for sure, he's not dead!" O'Neill swore, a terrified tone to his voice.

"What you gonna do now?" Thomas sneered, not liking the position he'd been forced into by none of his own doing.

"You can start by shutting your yap while I think this thing through," O'Neill said irritably. "He's out there and he's hurt. I know I hit him, so he can't have gone far!"

The sudden shock of the bullet threw Madigan to the ground with a crushing blow. For a time he lay there unable to move. The sun in his eyes forced him to close them while he gathered his thoughts. That he'd been shot he was sure, and the realization of it made him all the madder for being so careless.

Madigan doubted it was Indians that did the shooting. He had seen no sign of unshod ponies for the last two days, and the Navajo had been at peace with the white man for several years now. Of course, you could never rule out some renegades being loose in these parts, but they usually rushed you as a bunch.

As the initial shock quickly wore off, Madigan forced himself to his feet. The front of his shirt was soaked with blood and he felt unsteady. The buckskin was standing a few feet away, and Madigan staggered over to the horse. Whoever tried to kill him would not be long in trying to finish the job, so his only chance was to escape.

The shot had come from high up in the rocks. The way he figured it, the would-be killer, after watching to see if Madigan moved, was thinking he'd killed him with the first shot. More than not, the killer was on his way down to make sure.

The buckskin moved nervously toward his master, smelling the blood on Madigan's shirt. Taking hold of the saddle horn, it took all of Madigan's strength to pull himself into the saddle. Once there, the big horse moved off on his own accord, it being all Madigan could do just to stay on. The packhorse followed a short distance behind.

Fighting to stay conscious, Madigan vaguely heard hoofbeats in the distance, then nothing as a curtain of darkness fell over him.

Pete LaRue and his partner had been riding slowly through the twisting canyon floor when the distant sound of a rifle shot came echoing off the canyon walls.

"What do you make of that?" Shorty asked his friend.

"Maybe a hunter, although I haven't seen a deer track since we entered these canyons."

"Me either," Shorty replied matter-of-fact. "You think it might be O'Neill and the boys?"

"Who else would it be way out here? Nobody but fools be riding in this country," LaRue said, shaking his head in disgust.

Lightning cracked off in the distance. "Looks like we're in for a storm. Better find some shelter on high ground before it gets here," LaRue suggested.

The two men spurred their horses to a gallop, hoping to find an overhang of rock to shield them from the inevitable downpour. Finding such a place, they picketed the horses out of the elements before stretching out on their bedrolls to wait out the rain that was already upon them.

"At any rate," Shorty began, "the storm will wipe out our tracks. And since we haven't been keeping strictly to the trail, it'll make it hard for O'Neill to follow us, if that's what he's doing." The two men laughed at the thought of O'Neill left with nothing to follow.

"Course, he may not be following us at all," LaRue said seriously. "Didn't he say the gold was somewhere around here?"

"That's right," Shorty confirmed. "Now, about that gold. How do you propose we find it?"

LaRue thought for a moment. "I remember where the old prospector's cabin is. The prospector was killed less than a mile from it with an arrow the likes of nothing I've seen any Indian use before. The way I figure, the gold has got to be within a few miles of that spot. Why else would the old man have been killed? He prospected around these parts for years without any trouble, then the day he dies, he has a gold figurine clutched in his hand." LaRue stared off into the distance in deep thought. Finally he spoke again. "I think he stumbled onto the location of the treasure and was killed to keep its whereabouts secret."

"Could be," Shorty said, nodding his head in agreement. "But that doesn't tell me how we're going to find it for ourselves and at the same time keep our skins intact."

"I wish I knew," LaRue admitted. "I wish I knew."

The rain came down in a great deluge, and the two men pressed further back under the overhang to stay dry while the horses put their backs to the wind in an attempt to ward off the chill.

It was growing stormier and LaRue gathered some dead brush from a dry crevice in the rocks and made a small fire. Both men agreed that it was wise to make camp here for the night. They were soon settled in for the long hours ahead, while the rain beat a drumroll on the ground a few feet away.

Madigan came to again, barely clinging to the saddle. The big buckskin was stepping out slowly, picking his way through a trail bordered by huge boulders and strewn with rubble from crumbling rock. Blood slowly dripped down the front of Madigan's shirt and onto his leg, spreading out in a darkening stain.

Madigan's head swam in a sea of pain so intense he felt he could not go on any further, yet he had to. The survival instinct within him was strong, he could not give in to the pain any more than he would give in to the man who had shot him. Whoever it was would surely be on this trail trying to finish the job, and Madigan didn't want to stick around and give the bushwhacker another chance at him.

The ground opened up on both sides of the path as Madigan leaned over in the saddle to better stay on. Lightning flashed in the distance while the wind began to stir up some. It was evident a storm was brewing and Madigan felt a little relief knowing the rain would wash out his tracks. If only he could keep ahead of his pursuer long enough to let the rain do its work.

He rode on for several more miles before he felt the first raindrops upon his back. The wet coolness was refreshing and gave him new strength to ride on. The big horse beneath him sensed the urgency to find shelter and broke into a fast trot toward some rough-looking country ahead.

Coming to a dry creek bed, Madigan hesitated before crossing. The banks at either side were steep and it would be difficult for the packhorse to scale the far embankment. With the rain, it was only a matter of time before the roaring waters of a flash flood filled the creek to overflowing, taking everything caught in its path along with it. There would be little warning when the waters came, maybe a few seconds at best, no more.

Madigan agonized over the decision. If he started the horses across and the waters came upon them, there would be but seconds for them to get up and out the other side before being washed away to their doom. Madigan had little fear of the buckskin not making it. He was a powerful animal able to take care of himself, even with a load on his back.

It was the packhorse Madigan worried about. Loaded heavily with supplies, it might not be able to carry them up the other side. Still, if he could get to the other side, Madigan would be safe from anyone following as long as the rain held out. In his weakened state, he didn't have a prayer of fighting them off. He would have to try to make it across.

The rain increased in intensity as they slid down the stream side to the creek bottom already turning to a quagmire of slippery mud from the barrage of water falling from the heavens. The buckskin kept his footing, but the packhorse, top-heavy from the supplies on his back, was soon down and trying to scramble back to his feet.

Finally, after what seemed like an eternity, he was up and moving toward the far side of the stream, but not before Madigan heard the ominous sound of roaring water bearing down on them. Gritting his teeth against the pain, Madigan whirled the buckskin around behind the other animal and gave the packhorse a slap on its rump. The horse lurched ahead and made it halfway up the bank before losing its footing and sliding back to the creek bed.

Taking a quick look upstream, Madigan could see debris being thrown in the air from the surge of water crashing down from the mountains not far away. There was only one thing left for him to do: cut the pack loose and save the horse. Luckily, his Sharps, along with ammunition and a few other things he used every day, were tied in a smaller pack on top.

Grabbing loose the ties, Madigan pulled this pack in front of him while he cut the main pack from the animal's back letting it fall free. In a split second the two horses raced up the bank and a hundred yards beyond to freedom.

They were safe for the moment, and Madigan turned in his saddle in time to see a gigantic wall of water rush past where moments before they were trying, almost in vain, to climb out of its way. A great emotional release rose within him, over-shadowing the anger he felt at losing the supplies.

O'Neill and Thomas held their ground behind the large boulder they hoped would shield them from the onslaught of bullets they felt were sure to come.

"I know I hit him," O'Neill said as he turned to Thomas, expecting him to confirm what he himself was not sure of. "You saw him go down, didn't you?" he pleaded.

Thomas stared at O'Neill, who he was beginning to despise. O'Neill, the great leader, the one that was going to make them all rich or get them all killed. O'Neill the coward!

Thomas was no newcomer to violence, growing up in east Texas, the son of a card cheat and womanizer, his mother a drunk that often found herself waking up in the morning with a stranger. Finally, it was the wrong stranger and she wound up being beaten to death.

After she died, James and his father drifted from town to town playing the cheap dance halls of the cattle towns, keep-ing just ahead of the law. When James was twelve, his pa got caught dealing from the bottom of the deck by a big, raw-boned cowhand named Ed Piker. In an instant, the older Thomas lay dead on the floor, still clutching the card that cost him his life.

With his pa gone, James wandered from one cow camp to another learning the trade of the cowboy. He learned another thing too—how to handle a gun. Later he found there was more money to be made with a gun than punching cows, and he left the cowboy life for that of the gunslinger.

Now, years later, here he was, forced to back up a madman who he was sure wouldn't think twice about shooting him in the back if it would serve his purpose.

If I get out of this mess I'm in, I think I'll just keep riding, Thomas thought to himself before answering O'Neill.

"No, I didn't see anything, so I'll have to take your word for it." Thomas smiled inwardly at not giving O'Neill any satisfaction. O'Neill scowled but said nothing. Within minutes his life had changed from triumph to what very well could be tragedy.

Madigan was out there somewhere close by and he had the advantage of knowing exactly where the other two men were. O'Neill began to sweat. How did this happen?

One minute his enemy was in his sights, at O'Neill's mercy. Now it was the other way around and he wondered if he would live to see another day.

O'Neill glanced around nervously, trying to find a way out of the predicament he had gotten himself into. One side of the boulder he was behind lay up against a cliff that rose over a hundred feet straight up, blocking an escape in that direction.

In front, the ground lay flat, ringed by broken rock, large boulders, and crevices cut deep into the face of the cliff side opposite O'Neill's hiding place. From his viewpoint on top of the mesa, O'Neill knew that the canyon narrowed further on, making a perfect spot for an ambush if one so desired.

Considering this, his best chance for freedom would be a mad dash back the way he had come, hoping against all hope that surprise would be on his side. A man bursting out at a dead run might gain a few precious seconds, and those seconds might be all that would keep him alive.

Without warning, O'Neill swung to the saddle and spurred his mount out in the open. Laying over in the saddle to make a smaller target, he slapped leather to the charging animal and hung on, expecting the sound of gunfire at any second. None came.

James Thomas was not in the least bit shocked at being deserted by O'Neill. The man was a coward through and through. And like all yellow bellies, he would not think twice about betraying his friends. So O'Neill's actions were for the most part foreseeable.

Thomas did have to laugh at the sight of O'Neill hunched over the saddle, his big butt in the air as if it were some kind of shield to hide behind. Thomas thought about shooting O'Neill himself, then letting O'Neill try to explain to the others how he got a bullet in the butt.

As for James, he had taken all he was going to take and was about to ride out of the picture forever. He'd drift down El Paso way. The cowboy life wasn't a bad life and the company was a whole lot better.

The storm lasted through the night, lightning casting grotesque shadows on the walls and rocks around them, filling the hollow where LaRue and Shorty slept with mysterious dancing spirits of the night. The wind moaned over and through the rocks, singing a song of loneliness to the Navajo gods.

The small fire had long since gone out, leaving the coffee pot to get cold, while Shorty shivered, trying to sleep. Always the one to be cold even on the warmest of nights, he was now rolled up in his two wool blankets and freezing.

Lightning cracked, and Shorty sat up abruptly. Was it the noise of the lightning that woke him or was it something else? Times like these were the one thing Shorty could never get used to.

It wasn't the darkness around him that bothered him, he thought as he adjusted the blankets around his legs; it was the confounded damp, miserable nights he was forced to endure that were the worst.

He was just getting ready to roll over and go back to sleep when he was again startled awake. He listened, but wasn't really sure he had heard anything.

On nights like these a man's mind tends to wander, and he might believe he heard something when it was only the wind. It was no use trying to sleep, so he tossed the blankets aside and got to his feet.

Gathering a pile of sticks, he quickly built a small mound of wood for a fire, when a noise from the darkness again caught his attention.

He immediately froze, straining to hear. For a long minute he listened before he heard it again. He tried to remember what it reminded him of. Then it hit him. It was the sound of a dozen horses walking by in the night.

He should have known instantly. But with the wind and rain, it was hard to hear clearly. Yes, he was sure of it now. Somewhere close by, a small band of horses was moving by in the dark. Whether the horses had riders was impossible to tell and by morning their tracks would be washed clean by the rain.

Shorty peered into the night trying to see, but to no avail. Except for the occasional flashes of lightning, the night was just too black to see anything. Gathering a couple of small pebbles, he tossed them at his friend a few feet away.

"I'm awake," LaRue whispered.

"Did you hear them?"

LaRue came slowly to his feet and joined Shorty where he stood, gun in hand.

"What do you make of it?" LaRue asked.

Shorty thought for a moment, still straining for the slightest sound. All was quiet now.

"Sounded like maybe a dozen horses moving through," Shorty answered. "Beats me what they're up to. Horses usually seek shelter in weather like this."

"Indians?"

"Not likely. At least not this time of night. And from what I was led to believe, most of them don't ride horses in these parts. Could be wrong about the horses—wouldn't be the first time I was wrong. But then again, I never knew of Indians running together in such large numbers in the dark. They don't like to move around in the dark—something to do with the spirits of the dead out at night.

"Of course. If not Indians, who else could it be?" LaRue moved closer to his friend before hazarding an answer. "Could be the ones we're looking for."

"If it's them, we don't have far to look. It seems they've found us."

"The question is," LaRue said in a serious voice, "what do they intend to do with us, now that we have them right where they want us?"

"Or it could be O'Neill and his bunch," Shorty threw in. "It'd be just like him to make them ride all night, wet or dry."

"He's crazy enough for that," LaRue confirmed.

CHAPTER 12

It was several miles before O'Neill dared stop from his dash for freedom. He felt safe for the moment. Taking his canteen, he drank freely, wiping his mouth on his sleeve when finished, before replacing the cork in the container.

Taking a slow, hard look around, he was pleased with what he saw: a patchwork of jagged rock and canyons surrounded him which offered a multitude of hiding places.

The wind started to pick up and a coolness gripped the air. A few miles away lightning cracked, and thunder sounded like a thousand drums all beating at once.

O'Neill watched the storm advance toward him before riding up a small game trail that promised shelter in one of the numerous small caves in the area.

Finding the cave a suitable place to stay dry, he pulled out the fixins and rolled a smoke. Only then did he allow himself time to consider the fate of Thomas, still out there somewhere, maybe even dead, although O'Neill doubted it for he had heard no shots.

The rain started falling in huge driving sheets, and now and again the wind blew some mist into the mouth of the cave where O'Neill stood.

The cave had apparently been formed eons ago, when a prehistoric river flowed through this area and cut the deep canyons as it rushed on unerringly to some far-off, unseen ocean.

Lighting a match, he moved back deeper into the cave to escape the occasional blast of moisture. The light from the match was dim at best, but by holding it over his head, he was able to make out the fact that the cave was much bigger than he had first suspected.

A few yards in from the entrance the walls opened up, the ceiling going up and out of sight in the dim light. The match soon burned O'Neill's fingers and he was forced to drop it. Fumbling for another, he grew uneasy in the darkness, so he quickly walked out to the mouth of the cave again.

The storm intensified. Out in the open the wind was gusting to gale force. O'Neill dug around in his saddlebag and withdrew a thick candle. Seconds later, he was again moving deeper into the cave, the candle giving off twice the light of the match.

The floor of the cave was relatively flat and smooth, as if ground down by a huge grinding wheel. The walls were of red stone and also rather smooth to the touch.

O'Neill had entered fifty feet or more when something caught his attention on the wall ahead. There, some fifteen feet tall and twenty feet across, was a mural depicting Spanish priests holding crosses high overhead as they walked along with conquistadors on horseback guarding what appeared to be Indian slaves carrying baskets on their shoulders.

Standing there in the flickering light, O'Neill studied the picture in detail. To the best of his knowledge there had not been any Spanish conquistadors in this land for over three hundred years. Yet here before him in splendid color, seemingly as fresh as the day it was painted, was a graphic depiction of a time long ago, a time when Spanish conquistadors swept over the country like a plague in the quest for treasure held sacred by the natives.

One thing bothered him about the picture: it was his belief that the Spanish invaders hadn't strayed this far north, so what was the explanation for this wonderful sight before him?

He wiped his finger across the image, then looked to find a

light sheen of white-and-gold had rubbed off. Holding the candle closer he examined the mural more carefully. He was unable to identify what the white chalky substance was, but the other had the sparkle that only real gold had.

Whoever had painted this masterpiece, for a masterpiece it truly was, had used real gold for part of the coloring. O'Neill was astonished at this startling revelation. It could mean only one thing: he was closer than ever to his goal of getting the treasure.

A breeze filtered through from somewhere in the cave's interior, threatening to extinguish the flame. At the same time, a stream of hot wax ran down the short stub of candle causing O'Neill to switch the torch to the other hand.

Studying the fire, he realized that the tip of the flame bent outward in the direction of the cavern's entrance. Watching the flare, O'Neill pondered the significance of his discovery.

If the wind was blowing the flame outward, then the air had to be coming from someplace deep within the cave itself. And that could mean only one thing: there had to be another opening to allow the air in. Excitement stirred within O'Neill as he made his way outside.

The storm was in full fury as he reached the spot where he had picketed his horse, under an overhang of red sandstone a short distance from the cavern's threshold. Looking back over his shoulder, O'Neill observed the cave's gaping mouth, sinister in the growing darkness, like the mouth of a huge skull, ready to swallow a man up, never to see the light of day again.

The more he studied the black hole, the less he felt the need to go exploring until morning. Besides, Madigan was still out there somewhere, maybe close by, so O'Neill's best bet was to make a cold camp and wait for morning. In the morning he would make sure he was alone; then and only then would he take the time to explore further.

O'Neill's camp was north of the opening to the cave about fifty yards. In the blackness around him, he would be invisible to anyone more than ten feet from camp. And by making a cold camp, there would be no fire to give his position away. Only the occasional burst of lightning might reveal his hiding place, but O'Neill had little worry of that happening. A man would have to be looking directly at the camp when a flash occurred, and even then it was doubtful he could see anything, with the rain and all.

The wind covered up any noise he might inadvertently make, and by now his tracks would be a thing of the past, washed clean by the torrents of water.

O'Neill wasted no time getting into his bedroll, not even bothering to unsaddle his horse. Smug in the knowledge that he was safe for the night, he was soon fast asleep.

Around 3 a.m., he rose from his bed to let water. The wind was blowing fiercely and the rain was pelting down in great thundering waves.

Reaching for the flap on his saddlebag, O'Neill lifted it and withdrew from deep within an almost empty bottle of rotgut whiskey, appropriately named red-eye. Turning the bottle on end, he quickly drank the remainder, then threw the empty vessel away in the night.

Wiping his mouth on his sleeve, he let out a belch that pleased him, and he started to roll up again in his blankets when a movement in the darkness alerted him to possible danger. Was it just something blowing in the wind, or was there someone out there?

O'Neill silently came to his feet, so as not to give his position away. His horse stamped a foot nervously and blew a rush of air from its nostrils. O'Neill stood motionless, gun in hand, waiting for whatever was to come.

The horse stamped his hoof again and shied away from some unknown intruder still hidden in the moonless night. Straining to hear even the slightest of sounds, sweat running down his face burning his eyes, O'Neill waited, choking back panic.

Ten minutes that seemed like hours passed before O'Neill dared to move from his hiding place, then only with great trepidation did he proceed to the side of his horse. Thunder boomed in the distance and caused him to turn and look over his shoulder in alarm in time to see another flash of lightning that for a split second painted the landscape a ghostly-green-ish white.

With his hand on his animal's neck he could feel it shud-der in fear, so O'Neill started to speak to it in a reassuring voice when his attention was caught by a shadowy figure on the opposite side of the horse.

O'Neill froze, unable to move, hysteria raising in his throat. Then a great bolt of electricity split the night air and there before him, impelled on a stick, was the head of a man whose eyes were ripped out, blood still fresh from the wounds dripping down his cheeks. The mouth was opened in an eter-nal scream, nothing but a hollow where the tongue had once been.

A sudden piercing scream shattered the night as O'Neill bolted backward in his uncontrolled scramble to be away from this ghastly apparition from hell. In his backward dash, he tripped and fell hitting his head on the rock-hard ground. Knocked unconscious by the blow, O'Neill lay there, his body not moving while the demons of his mind watched on in amusement.

"Man, that's weird," Tom Cook said, shaking his head in disbelief. "What ya suppose happened to him?"

"Something bad, that's for sure. A man's hair doesn't turn snow white like that for no reason, and did you see his eyes?"

"Yeah, like there's nothing inside. They just look at you like you're not even there. Man, I'm tellin' you, this whole thing's got me spooked."

Tom poked at the log on the fire with a long twig, causing sparks to fly into the night. Both men watched as the bright specks climbed higher in the evening sky before winking out.

"Who found him?" the man sitting with Cook asked.

"Jackson and a few of the others. When O'Neill and Jim

didn't show up after three days, Jackson took a couple of the boys and went looking. Only found O'Neill and he ain't talked yet. Just keeps staring straight ahead not saying anything."

"Anyone going out looking for Jim?"

"Some of the boys are going out in the morning. Going to try to backtrack O'Neill to wherever he left his horse. Shouldn't be too hard. The way he was stumbling around out there, he couldn't have gone far." The two men gazed into the flames of the fire lost in thought for a long while.

"With the storm gone, it would be easy to find his tracks, being any others would be washed clean by the rain from the night before."

"Wonder what they'll find?" Tom said abruptly, startling his friend from his thoughts.

The next morning, several of the men rode out looking for Jim Thomas. It was easy to follow the tracks made by O'Neill in his confused stumbling walk across the flats. The rain had cleansed the land of all signs of trespass up to the end of the storm, leaving a clear imprint of O'Neill's aimless passing.

In a short time the men came upon the remains of Thomas on the pole. His body was nowhere to be seen, and the men didn't feel like venturing into any of the caves that were so common in the area to look for it. Finding O'Neill's dapple gray a short distance away, they gathered what they could in a hurry and rode off after burying the head of James Thomas, the cowboy who was going to go home.

For two days they stayed in camp and waited for O'Neill to come to his senses. Another storm blew through and brought more rain to the land. A land that normally looked baked and dry now took on a brilliant coat of colors as all sorts of wild flowers bloomed to show their gratitude for the life-giving water from above.

Even O'Neill slowly regained his composure and came back to the land of reality. It was on the third day after O'Neill returned to camp, while the men were sitting around the noon fire eating. Since O'Neill's return, the men had been taking turns feeding him and more or less helping him with other things much like they would a small child.

It now became Warren Elegant's turn to feed O'Neill his noon meal. Elegant was a miserable little twit, with a mouth befitting a man twice his size, and his curly black hair bushed out from under his hat, giving the impression of someone with a dirty rat's nest on his head. In his career he had been a town clerk, tax collector, and embezzler. In truth, he was nothing more than an imbecile of the lowliest order.

Always complaining and trying to get others to do his work, he was now confronted with the disagreeable task of tending to O'Neill. Elegant had always been afraid of O'Neill and men like him, being the natural coward that he was. But now seeing the terrified form of O'Neill before him brought out what little courage the man possessed.

"I'm not going to feed this idiot! If he wants to eat he can feed himself!" Elegant said with a sneer.

"Aren't ya afraid he'll hear you talking like that?" Dave Donoven hissed with that big Irish grin he always displayed when he was egging someone on.

"Afraid of him?" Elegant swore, his face turning crimson in a fit of rage. "I wasn't afraid of him when he was all here, so why should I be afraid of him now?" the little coward lied.

The men standing around the camp began to laugh at the enraged man before them.

"You're afraid of your shadow, little man, so sure as hell you're afraid of O'Neill in the shape he's in or not!" Donoven threw in, the grin still on his face.

"I am not!" Elegant screamed as he stepped forward and slapped O'Neill full in the face as hard as he could. Stunned silence filled the air at the sight of Elegant's despicable actions.

Taking this to mean a sign of approval rather than pity, the little man raised his hand ready to strike again. He was determined to hit O'Neill hard enough to knock him over this time as his first blow failed to do so. Gathering up all his strength, he swung with all the power he could muster. But to everyone's astonishment, O'Neill's left hand darted up and caught Elegant's hand while it was still in full swing, bringing it to an abrupt halt in midair.

"You're a dead man!" came O'Neill's voice through half-parted lips as his right hand reached across and caught hold of Elegant's eight-inch skinning knife, slowly withdrawing it from its sheath. In one quick motion, the knife slid up under Elegant's shirt and deep into his flesh. There was a gush of blood as a gurgling sound escaped from somewhere deep within Elegant's throat.

O'Neill had returned from the pits of hell a changed man. Before his ordeal, he was a coward sending others to do his dirty work, always trying to keep himself away from possible harm. Now he had returned a man of a different character, as the men would soon find out. You might even say the devil himself had returned in O'Neill's place.

CHAPTER 13

With the imminent danger behind him, Madigan relaxed a little. The flow of blood from his wound had slowed, but the pain was still tearing at him with a vengeance. He brought the buckskin to a halt and took the time to pack the wound with a piece of cloth cut from an extra shirt. He then soaked the cloth with whiskey from his saddlebag to sterilize it the best he could. The wound burned like hell fire when he pushed the cloth into the bullet hole, and he yelled so loud he almost frightened the horses away.

The sky was growing darker by the minute and he could smell the pungent odor of electricity in the air. He was still on the flats, and with the lightning dancing around him, it was no place to be. As the devil's light cracked at his back, Madigan hightailed it for a small canyon, where he hoped to find an overhang of rock to dry out in and rest from the ordeal of the day.

What he found, as he edged through a small opening in the rocks he'd seen only by chance, was more than a man could ever expect. Before him, a small canyon opened up with high stone walls on three sides, protecting an area of about two acres.

To one side, next to the canyon wall, almost hidden in the rocks, was a small cabin. It was easy to see that it was empty, at least for the time being. A thick layer of dust covered the porch with nothing having disturbed it for some time, save for a rabbit or two who in their scampering left their prints.

Along one side of the cabin was a corral into which Madigan led the horses. Behind the cabin was a small spring. The spring seeped through one corner of the corral, keeping the grass lush and green and providing plenty of drinking water for the horses.

Heavy shutters with gun slits were closed over the windows of the cabin. Dirt was carefully spread over the roof to prevent Indians from starting fires with fire arrows from on top of the shear cliffs which stood to the sides and back of the building. The roof hung over far enough to block arrows from reaching the walls of the little cabin from above. Whoever built it wanted a fort as much as a cabin.

The horses went right to work on the grass, and Madigan could see they would have plenty to eat and drink for the next few days, if he had to stay that long. Taking a careful look around and not realizing how weak he was, he staggered, more than walked, to the porch and up to the door. The latch string was out, so with a gentle tug he raised the inside latch and pushed on the door.

With a creak the door slowly opened to reveal the cabin's dark, musty interior. A single table with a candle on it stood in the middle of the one room. A cot was pushed against the far wall and some mining tools were stacked in one corner.

On a shelf stood tins of food, and he noticed that many more cans were open and lay empty, indiscriminately thrown across the floor. What caught Madigan's interest the most was the cot, and he quickly made his way to it and immediately fell asleep.

Sometime during the night, he awoke to find himself drenched in sweat and the pain in his chest throbbing like he'd been kicked by a mule. With a sense of fear, Madigan realized he was in the grip of a fever, and given his location miles from any help, he would almost certainly die.

He chuckled at the irony of it. Here he was, all alone in the middle of nowhere, in some long forgotten cabin about to meet his Maker when many men, Indians and white men alike, tried so hard and so long to put him under, and now a lousy fever was doing the job they miserably failed at.

He'd little fear for the horses, for he knew that as the grass gave out they could easily jump the fence of the little corral to freedom. Taking everything into account, Madigan closed his eyes and drifted off to sleep, at peace with himself and the world for the first time in his adult life.

Several hours later he was awakened by a noise and the feeling that something was being pushed deep within his chest. Surprisingly he felt little pain as the probing continued. There was a bitter taste in his mouth, and his lips felt numb. He opened his eyes and found a beautiful girl bending over him while an older woman stood beside her holding a small bowl in her hands. From time to time she would place the bowl at his lips and trickle a little of the foul-tasting liquid into his mouth, forcing him to swallow it.

With a gentle pull, the girl withdrew something from his chest and held it up to the coal-oil lantern hung on a nail overhead.

"I've got the bullet out," she said as she stroked Madigan's forehead with her other hand. Then she smiled as their eyes met and held for an instant. "The drink will keep the pain away and you will sleep," she said.

"Who are you?" Madigan asked, her face vaguely familiar, although in the delirium of the fever he probably couldn't recognize his own face.

"I am Lewana and this is my friend Mila," she said softly. "When you are better, you will remember us. For now you must sleep."

Madigan's eyes grew heavy as he fought in vain to stay awake. Something about the girl and her friend gnawed at the back of his mind, but before he could figure it out he was lost to the world.

Outside a coyote sang to the night gods, while on the rim high above the cabin, an Indian warrior sat cross-legged in silent vigil, the golden disk hanging from a silver chain around his neck reflecting the starlight of the inky-black sky overhead.

LaRue and Shorty cautiously rode out the next morning. It was hard to know whether they were being watched or not. The air smelled washed and clean as they made their way along the canyon bottom, heading ever westward while keeping an eye out for anything that looked of trouble. Nothing stirred except for an occasional jackrabbit.

Neither man spoke of the visitors in the night, but each knew that it was the foremost thing on each of their minds. Whoever it had been was in a big hurry to get somewhere or they would not have been riding in the middle of the night. At any rate, LaRue and his friend hadn't seen hide nor hair of anyone since daybreak, and both were glad of that fact.

About midmorning, the two men rode out from between two vertical walls of rock to be presented with a wide valley that stretched vastly out below them. Partway across was a stream reflecting sunlight from the torrents of water overflowing its banks from the rain of the night before.

"That stream was dry when I crossed it last. May be a while before we can get over, with the water so high," LaRue said, wiping the sweat from his brow. "Maybe by the time we get there, it'll be low enough to ford. I figure we're still a half-day's ride away."

Shorty nodded in agreement, saying nothing, his mind still on the events of the night.

A short time later, as they topped a small knoll, they spotted a cloud of dust to the north of them.

"Looks like nine, maybe ten riders. Maybe we ought to get out of sight," LaRue said. "Probably O'Neill and his bunch." Reining their horses around, they ducked into a small arroyo.

"I don't think they saw us," LaRue said when they were well hidden.

"Now we know who our visitors were last night."

"Most likely, the way they were going hell-bent-for-leather. Where do you suppose they're heading in such an all-fired hurry?" Shorty asked.

"Beats me. Just as long as they keep going away from us is all I care about," LaRue answered gravely.

"By the way, just where are we heading?" Shorty wanted to know. "I've been meaning to ask you, but there just didn't seem to be the right time till now."

"We are going to the cabin I told you about, the prospector's cabin where I stayed for a while. When we reach it we'll get our bearings and start looking from there."

"How are we going to find it again? Mighty big territory out here and you said it was well hidden."

"It is, but when I left, I marked a trail in such a way so I'd be able to follow it, but no one else could. All we have to do is keep our eyes out for a tall rock chimney. Should be able to see it for miles. The trail starts at the base of it."

Several hours later they spotted the chimney in the distance and rode for its base, only stopping long enough to allow the water to drain further before chancing to cross the swollen creek. Hours later, just after dark, they arrived at the cleft in the rock that marked the entrance to the hidden cabin. Not wanting to take any chances, they picketed their horses out of sight and walked the short distance to where they could scout the cabin without being seen.

LaRue was the first to suspect they weren't alone. "Look over toward the corral," he said, pointing to a spot beside the cabin. "There's movement, maybe a horse."

"Or maybe a deer. You did tell me this cabin wasn't known by anyone but you and the old prospector, and he's dead," Shorty reminded LaRue.

The buckskin, having picked up the two men's scent, let out a low warning.

"I guess somebody else knows about it now," said LaRue nervously. "Let's hope he's friendly."

Madigan awoke with a start that made his head hurt. Waiting for his eyes to clear, he choked back the urge to sit up until he was sure of his surroundings. Was it his imagination or did he hear the buckskin give a warning? First thing Madigan noticed was the women were gone and the lantern was out, leaving only the light of the moon filtering in through a crack in the shutters to see by.

Swinging his feet to the floor, Madigan tested his strength before trying to stand. Reaching down, he felt for his gun belt and buckled it around his waist, then checked to be sure it was loaded. It was, except for the empty chamber he, like all cowboys, usually kept under the hammer. Slipping a cartridge from his belt, he dropped it into the empty hole and closed the loading gate.

Madigan wasn't looking for any more trouble, but if it came his way he would be as ready as he could under the circumstances.

The way the cabin was built sitting back of the little canyon, there was only one way that any riders could come from. He peered through the crack between the shutters but could see no movement—not unusual, given the limited view from his position.

Somewhere in the darkness a horse snickered, answered by Madigan's own buckskin. So, there was somebody out there after all. Overhead a cloud drifted across the moon, and the land grew dark without the moonlight, making it impossible for Madigan to see if anyone approached the cabin.

He was in a dangerous situation and he knew it. His only chance was to take whoever was out there by surprise.

Moving slowly from the weakness, Madigan made his way to the small back window and crawled out without making a sound. As long as the moon stayed hidden he would be just as hard to see as they were to him.

He slowly inched his way to the corner of the cabin, listening for any sound out of place in the night. He was just easing up to the front corner when the moon slid out from behind the cloud, bathing everything in greenish light. Madigan froze, knowing that any movement on his part would give him away for sure.

Madigan wasn't the only one caught off guard. There in front of him facing the porch was a big man holding a gun. Beside him was a boy, or at least Madigan thought it was a boy from his size. They hadn't seen him yet.

"How about layin' those guns on the ground," Madigan ordered.

Neither of them moved for what seemed like minutes, and feeling the way he was, Madigan wasn't sure he could make much of a fight if they chose to go that way.

"Anything you say, partner," the big man said as they slowly bent over and laid their guns carefully on the ground. "Didn't mean you any harm," the big man said. "Last time I was here the place was deserted. Man can't be too careful out here."

Madigan covered them as he moved around the corner in full view. "Seems to me you took an awful chance coming up to the cabin the way you did. You left yourself open for someone to get the drop on you."

"We weren't hunting any trouble," the big man replied.

"Then why'd you sneak up to the cabin without hailing it first?"

The boy turned toward Madigan and for the first time, Madigan realized he was not a boy at all, but a very small man.

"We ran into trouble back on the trail and weren't sure who we might meet up with. You can see our point for being cautious. We just wanted to make sure it wasn't any of the bunch that's been trailing us, that's all," the little man said.

Well, maybe they were tellin' the truth and maybe they weren't. The main thing was that Madigan had gotten himself into a fix he couldn't see an easy way out of. If he'd not been wounded, he would have the time to hear them out and get a feeling for if they were telling the truth. But even as Madigan stood there he could feel his legs start to weaken and was having a hard time keeping the gun up.

Why, Madigan thought to himself, did everything have to happen to him? He'd started for California not bothering anyone and not wanting to be bothered by anyone. Just a peaceful ride, seeing the country, doing a little fishing along the way, mayhap a bit of huntin'. But life has a way of changing the best-laid plans. Usually, it only threw you a few problems along the way to make things interesting, or annoying at most, although Madigan could honestly say this was not one of those times. In the space of a few weeks he'd almost been blown up, chased from here to hell and back, and finally shot, not to mention the men he had to kill.

Now Madigan was saddled with the added problem of trying to figure out what to do with two men that could be friend or foe and he had no way of tellin' which. Of course, he could just shoot them on the spot and deal with his conscience later. Just thinking of it made Madigan realize that he must still be half out of his head. As it was, the decision was taken out of Madigan's hands.

Standing there with his gun covering the two men, he suddenly became aware of a strange look on their faces. Then everything seemed to turn upside down as if he was being drawn down into a deep whirlpool from which there was no escape.

Around and around he went, deeper and deeper into the void, the faces of the men growing wider and wider until they stretched themselves into grotesque masks. Was he seeing the face of death? Then . . . blackness. No sound, no pain, just total blackness. The blackest black Madigan had ever seen.

The first thing Madigan remembered was a flash of light, then blackness again. Next came a blast of sound as if the whole world was crashing in on him. Madigan's hand tightened on the gun, but it wasn't there. Slowly, ever so slowly, his senses crept back to him. The blackness turned to gray, then brown.

Noises kept entering his head to bounce back and forth in indiscernible patterns. At last a word filtered through, then another and another. "He's coming to," someone said.

A smell drifted by and Madigan's stomach growled.

"He'll be hungry when he wakes up," another voice from some distant place said.

It seemed like hours, days, before his mind cleared enough to open his eyes. When he did, Madigan found himself lying back on the cot. What's that smell, he wondered, not quite able to make out what it was yet.

Madigan felt a coolness on his forehead. A hand came into view and lifted a damp rag from him, and a drop of water fell into his eye. He blinked and his vision cleared some more, enabling him to see the big man sitting by his side on a chair that looked too small for the man.

"Well, you're back to the land of the living, I see," the big man said.

"Who are you?" Madigan asked weakly.

"You rest a while, then we'll talk," the big man said with a gentle smile. "When you feel up to it, we'll fix you something to eat."

Madigan must have dozed off, for when he awoke there was the smell of stew cooking. Seeing him awake, the two men came over and asked if he was strong enough to eat at the table. Madigan was, so they helped him to the table, where a bowl of hot stew and a cup of coffee waited. Over food they made friendly conversation.

Madigan found out the big man's name was Pete LaRue and the other went by the name of Shorty. Both were well educated and seemed friendly enough, but deep down he'd the feeling they were hiding something.

"You both seem to be honest men," Madigan said at long last, looking from one to the other, "but I feel there's something you left out."

The two men glanced at each other as if caught in an embarrassing situation, then seemed to reach an unspoken agreement.

"Speaking of honesty," LaRue said, suddenly growing uneasy, "we were part of the bunch that tried to kill you a few weeks ago." LaRue looked down at his hands nervously, beads of sweat broke out on his forehead. "In fact, I was the leader. For reasons that are now not even clear to me, I allowed those men to try to gun you down. Please believe me when I say there has not been a day gone by since that I have not regretted it.

Coming to his feet, the big man came to Madigan's side. "Shorty didn't have anything to do with it. He's just along for the ride, you might say. When you're well again, if you want to have me pay for my actions, I'll give you more than a fair chance at my hide. You deserve more, but that's all I have at present."

"Was it one of you that shot me?"

"Not us. We're not ambushers. So, like I said, if you want a chance at my hide I won't blame you."

"Thanks," was about all Madigan could think to say, but he knew deep in his heart that the three of them would be friends. They were all too much alike not to be. Revenge would serve no purpose.

"How many of your boys did I get with the big bruiser?" Madigan asked.

"You mean that buffalo gun of yours? Madigan nodded his head. "Two out on the plains. But, all told, you cost me five men, although two of them weren't your doing."

"What do you mean?" Madigan asked fully expecting the answer.

"Sent a couple after you with several horses to run you down."

"Smart move on your part."

"I thought so too. Only trouble was, they ran smack into a big old grizzly while it was feeding or wounded, I don't know which. Guess he didn't take too kindly to them intruding, so he made a meal of both of the men!

"Only thing I couldn't figure out was why they got off their horses and went into the brush where the bear was, unless it scared the horses so bad they threw the riders. Could have happened so fast the grizzly killed them the second they hit the ground.

"Never really know how, but sure makes me have a lot of respect for those big bears. Be glad you didn't have to see it. Those men were a mess. Believe me, it was gruesome."

"I did see it!"

LaRue gave Madigan a startled look. "How?"

"I set it up so the men would take cover in the brush where the bear was. I chanced to see them coming right after I'd a run-in with the grizzly, so I worked my way around it, then waited for your men." Madigan took in a deep breath as he remembered how he shook at the sight of the bear attack.

"When your men came hell-bent-for-leather around the corner, I was in the middle of the trail with my rifle pointed at them. Natural thing for a man to do is dismount and run for cover. That's just what they did, only the bear was waiting for them.

"So you see, both of us will have to live with the regret of our actions for the rest of our lives. So unless you have a mind to, just forget about a showdown between us," Madigan said sadly. "Now, how about some more stew, and fill it up this time. That stuff makes a man's belly cry out for more. By the way, if you don't mind me askin', what happened to the rest of your men?"

LaRue shot a glance at his partner and Madigan knew he'd hit a sore spot, but it was too late to take back the question.

"Renegade named O'Neill talked them into joining him."

At O'Neill's name, Madigan's blood ran cold. So he was out there waiting and he had a gang with him now. Madigan thought of the attempt to kill him with the dynamite, and all of a sudden it dawned on him that it must have been O'Neill that shot him. Who else would have shot and left a man lying there without checking to see if he was dead? Then Madigan remembered the two women he'd saved and what O'Neill would do to them if he had gotten his hands on them. Somehow Madigan had to find a way to stop him, not just for what O'Neill did to him, but . . . for her.

O'Neill quickly took charge of his men, many of whom were still stunned by what they'd just witnessed with the killing of Elegant. Looking from one man to the next, he seemed to be seeing into their very souls, and each man knew that there would be no turning back from this madman. You either followed him to the depths of hell or you died from his hand; there would be no other choice. Live or die, it was no longer their decision to make. Whatever reason they'd come along in the first place no longer mattered. They were completely under the will of this one man. From now on he would think for them and they would follow as of one mind. His control was absolute.

CHAPTER 14

The day dawned cold and clear as though washed by a giant waterfall before being dried out by the first ragged multicolored rays of the sun. O'Neill had barked out his orders for the men to break camp before the last stars reluctantly faded from the morning sky. Now they were saddled and ready to ride.

"We ride until we find the cave where I was camped," he growled as the men started out. "Any man try to cross me and I'll kill him no matter where he tries to hide on the face of the earth!"

His statement was irrational, but fear has a way of dulling the logical thought processes. And even though it would be an easy escape, fear gripped the men to their very depths so that it was as if their rabid leader held some mystical power over them, a strange magic they could neither hide from nor resist.

Just after dusk, they found the cave, sinister in the growing darkness, wind whistling from its mouth like a wailing banshee from hell, totally unnerving everyone but O'Neill, who took obvious delight in watching the men's reaction to the place.

"Make camp here and at first light, I'll show you where this hole leads to," O'Neill announced in a voice so eerie it made the hair on the back of a man's neck stand on end. An hour later the men sat around the campfire in small groups talking amongst themselves while O'Neill sat alone by the cave entrance waiting for first light.

About twenty minutes later, Donoven nudged the man next to him. "Do you smell that?" he asked, taking another sniff of the air like a hound on the trail of a raccoon.

"Yeah, what do you make of it? Smells like roasting chicken to me. Can't really tell, but one thing's for sure—it's hot food a cookin'."

"I was thinkin' the same thing. But where the heck's it comin' from?"

None of the men had eaten anything but beans and bacon with a little hardtack thrown in for some time, and little by little the aroma of the hot food was getting to each of them. Donoven came to his feet and cautiously started walking from one side of the camp to the next, all the while acutely aware of O'Neill's gaze following him. Donoven kept sniffing the air as he walked, like a hungry grizzly trying to locate a carcass that was ripening in the sun.

Finally he stopped and faced in the direction of the cave. But before he could say anything, O'Neill looked up from his bedroll next to the cave mouth and spoke in a quiet but commanding voice. Even though it was not much more than a whisper, it rang on the men's ears like thunder.

"The smell is coming from the cave."

A hush fell upon the camp at O'Neill's words as the men realized the truth of the statement. The smell was indeed coming from the cave. But who could it be? If it was Indians, then why not a guard at the cave's opening? These questions and many more flooded the men's minds as they sat there in silence, fear capturing their minds once more.

"Now you know why I had to find this cave," came O'Neill's voice, barely louder than before. "It is the entrance to a hidden valley, a valley that will change all of our lives forever."

The shock of this statement showed on each man's face as the excitement stirred them to life again. Could this man, this monster they were now forced to follow, be telling the truth? And if he was, how did he know? How could he possibly know what was in that cave?

O'Neill was now on his feet and came quickly into the light of the campfire. After some thought, he turned toward the rest of the men and addressed them.

"You think I'm crazy, that I've gone loco, you lazy trash of the earth. You ask yourselves how could I possibly know where the cave leads to." O'Neill looked each man in the eye before continuing. "When you found me on the desert, you figured I had wandered out there to escape whoever killed Thomas.

"I heard some of you say I was insane when you found me. Maybe so, but I think not! I know what is in the valley because I have been there! I have seen where they keep the gold and I have felt their mark upon my very soul!"

As the men watched wide-eyed, O'Neill took a firm hold of his shirt and tore it open to reveal a hideous burn across his chest. The men, most being cowboys, had at one time or another branded cattle and knew the unmistakable mark that a red-hot iron makes on flesh: the grisly puffed up skin, the red-black scar tissue, and blue-green scab that forms inch by inch to protect the new skin as it forms underneath. That he had been to hell, they all now agreed. But was hell at the other end of this tunnel, or was it their destiny?

It was Donoven who first broke the silence. "How were you able to get away from the ones who did that to you?" he asked suspiciously.

O'Neill let a sinister smile cross his face. "When they put the hot iron to my flesh," he said, letting the effect of his words soak in, "I pretended to pass out.

"When they thought I was out, they relaxed their hold on me. It was then I pulled a derringer out of my boot and shot one of them through the head. I took the other one hostage and made him show me where the cave went. After I saw, I made him lead me out again."

"But how'd you get away from the others?" Donoven asked.

"It was dark, and I didn't see any others. When we reached the mouth of the tunnel, I cut the man's throat and hid him in the rocks. He's right over there, if any of you want to have a look," he said, pointing to a spot where a small ravine ran off in the darkness. "Then a fever must've took hold of me, cause the next thing I remember was someone hit me in the face. You know the rest." O'Neill purposely left out the part about being scared half out of his wits at seeing the head of Thomas.

At first light the men were gathered 'round the campfire, trying to keep warm in the frigid desert wind. Soon the sun would warm the ground and surrounding rock faces, and they, in turn, would warm the air. But each man knew that long before the day's chill burned off, they would be deep in the bowels of the earth seeking either their fortune or their death.

To everyone's surprise, O'Neill insisted that no one stay with the horses, let alone stand guard at the cave's opening. Maybe he didn't feel the need for it—or was the real reason that he didn't want to give any man the chance to escape? One could only guess at his thinking. So it was that every last man went into the cave while the horses were left tied outside by a small trickle of water, where they could help themselves if need be.

The extra supplies were hidden in the rocks, both from the heat of the day and from any wandering animal that might decide to make lunch from the extra food packs.

Nervous was not the word for what the men felt as they entered that black foreboding hole in the side of the cliff. There was no backing out for any of them. O'Neill saw to that as he stood just outside watching the men blindly go through the entrance one by one until the last man disappeared in the darkness.

A few feet inside, the first man lit his torch, which had been prepared for the occasion the night before. Instantly the interior was illuminated in yellowish light and the men were astounded at the vastness of the cavern. As the flickering light fell on the huge mural, the men gasped in amazement, for O'Neill had not mentioned a word of the painting to any of them.

For the moment, the men were caught up in the sight of the painting. Even O'Neill had to stare in wonder, for he had only seen a small portion of the mural at a time, as he had only the light of a candle to see by. Now, as a second and third torch were lit, the full majesty of the painting displayed itself before them in all its glory.

And glory it was. There were reds, golds, and yellows more brilliant than any found in the real world. A patch of blue reminded O'Neill of the bluebirds he watched as a child on his father's farm back East. How these colors survived all these years was anyone's guess, but here they were.

In a sudden flash of guilt or conservation (no one could tell) O'Neill ordered the men with the torches to step back so the smoke would not harm the mural. His concern for the mural had completely taken the men by surprise, for it was not his usual character to worry of such things.

Soon the men were on the move again, cautiously moving along in the darkness, not knowing what lay ahead of them. From time to time a man would trip and fall, cussing at the unseen obstacle that had fallen him in the dark while the flickering light of the torches served to blind the men as well as light their way. And so it was that they walked deeper into the cave.

Whenever a man would trip and fall, he would be jeered by his friends for being clumsy, and the whole procession would have to come to a halt while the man regained his feet. It almost became a game with the men, each waiting to see who would be the next victim of their insults.

Charlie Scott, a short, round man with ruddy complexion and a gripe for everything, was walking a few feet in front and slightly to the side of the lead torch man when he went down like a ton of bricks. The laughter started immediately, followed by the usual verbal abuse bestowed on those unfortunate enough to take a spill.

"Get to yer feet, you clumsy oaf!" Donoven sneered.

Scott didn't move. Urging Scott to his feet, the men became dismayed when he still failed to rise. Upon further investigation, the truth was revealed. There sticking out of Scott's forehead was the shaft of an arrow. The chronic complainer hadn't known what hit him.

In a heartbeat, the men scattered for cover, flinging the torches away from them in their mad scramble so as to make as hard a target as possible, each man using what little cover he could find. All of them except O'Neill, who stood his ground dimly illuminated by the glow of a torch thrown down a few feet from him.

O'Neill appeared ghost-like standing there, his white hair blowing softly in the current of air that had been growing stronger as they moved deeper into the cave. Nothing moved, not the men or O'Neill. No one even dared breathe. Then, in the blackness ahead, a low drawing sound was heard, quickly followed by the explosive roar of O'Neill's Colt. In the confines of the tunnel, the explosive roar of the gun was deafening, and it would be several minutes before the men were able to hear again.

When they again dared lift their heads to look around, they were shocked to find that O'Neill was gone! The men, overcome by panic, clung to the cave floor in the dim light of the single torch that still burned. No noise was heard, save the breathing of the men and an occasional nervous cough. What seemed like minutes passed; then in desperation someone asked the question that was on everyone's mind.

"Where the hell is O'Neill? What should we do now?"

"You might try waiting for my orders!" came the reply from O'Neill out of the darkness ahead.

In seconds O'Neill reappeared dragging the corpse of a man behind him. The torches were quickly relit, and the men gathered round the dead man.

"He's some kind of Indian," Jack Ward said as he peered at the body, "but none the likes of any I've seen."

The body before them was that of a man in his mid-forties, yet he had the physique of someone in his early twenties. He was muscular and tanned the color of rich bronze. His hair was cut short and well trimmed, not like the usual Indians who liked to leave their hair long about their shoulders.

The bow with which the man was armed was not like any the men had ever seen before. Made of wood, it had a handle made of some type of metal that shined in the light from the torches. And the wood that made up the limbs of the weapon was made of several layers of flat wood carefully fitted together so as to fit as one, each piece being a shade of color different from the other. An attractive weapon to be sure.

Apache John, a half-breed saddle tramp that had joined O'Neill's gang in Durango, came forward, stooped over, and picked the bow up. After examining it for some time, he slowly brought it up and tried its pull.

Now, Apache John was known to have used a bow for a good part of his life, and when he spoke of the weapon he held in his hands, he spoke with some authority.

"I'd say she pulls about sixty-five pounds," he started. "Enough to give it a range greater than three hundred yards with the right arrow. And looking at the arrow in Charlie there, I'd say it's matched pretty well to the bow."

"What tribe makes it?" O'Neill asked quietly of the half-breed, even though O'Neill knew John wouldn't be able to answer. He had asked it as much to make a point as anything, figuring every man there would be straining to hear the answer.

"None I know of," came the reply. "But I'll tell you one thing. This here bow is a work of art, the way it's built. There ain't an Indian I've ever known could even start to build it. No, sir. Whoever built this knows more about wood than any Indian alive. Look at how the wood's joined. It looks like one piece instead of four," he said passing the bow amongst the men clustered around him. "From the looks of this, it will not be easy to take them! These people are thinkers and they already know we are here and what we're looking for."

"Look at the headband he's wearing! It's solid gold!" someone yelled, pointing to the dead man at their feet.

Suddenly the men were in a frenzy trying to grab the golden band before any of their friends could snatch it.

"The first man to lay hands on that headband will be buried with it," O'Neill stated flatly. "There will be plenty for all of us later. I'll not have you fighting like a pack of dogs over this trifling little piece of junk. Now get walking! Donoven, you take the lead!" he ordered. There was dead silence as the men continued on through the tunnel.

He called that headband junk, Donoven thought as he led the way into the blackness, a torch held high in one hand while his other hand felt along the cool stone wall. That junk could keep me in money for months, yet O'Neill made us leave it there. He's crazy, or there's an awful lot of gold ahead, he surmised as he cautiously walked along.

The more Donoven thought about the riches that lay ahead, the more careless he became. Maybe it was his Irish blood or maybe just the promise of wealth, but soon he was moving ahead in strides that were impossible for the men behind him to follow. Curiously, O'Neill said nothing to hold him back.

Sweat was breaking out on Donoven's forehead as he almost ran along, slowing only enough to allow his torch to stay lit. Nevermind that there might be an ambush waiting ahead, his mind was now fully possessed by the gold fever and nothing or no one could stop him until he got what he was after.

When the great swiveling rock shuddered, then tilted slightly downward beneath his feet, Donoven was taken completely off guard. Stopping in his tracks, he listened for any telltale sign of what was happening. He felt something give, but in the darkness one's sensations often belie what is really happening. With the flickering torchlight and only the sound of the men walking behind him, it would be easy to imagine something that wasn't real.

Slowly he took another step forward. Everything felt solid—no movement, no noises. Another step with the same results. Smiling at himself for thinking something was amiss, he shifted the torch to the other hand and took another confident step. It was then that all hell broke loose.

In the midst of a great grinding roar, Donoven flung himself flat to the ground. Beads of sweat broke out on his forehead as he tried desperately to find something, anything, to grab hold of. Panic welled up in his stomach as the reality of what was happening surged through his mind. There was nothing to get a hold on—not a crack, crevice, nothing!

He tried in desperation to dig his fingernails into the unyielding rock, but it was useless. As the floor tilted more and more, his body slipped faster toward the abyss below, just the eerie grating of his fingernails on the stone could be heard as he slid closer to the edge.

In less than a second it was too late for him to save himself. As the rock pivoted on its center, Donoven dropped feet first into the deep void below. By the time he hit bottom he had crashed head over heels into the rough stone sides a half-dozen times or more.

Yet, the loudest sound heard was that of his body hitting bottom with a sickening crunch. Not even then did any sound escape Donoven's lips. He was not the kind to cry out in fear, not even in death.

As the great stone slowly righted itself, two streaks of blood and a piece of cloth were the only signs that Donoven had passed this way. The two narrow lines of blood, about two feet long, ended as abruptly as they had begun. The cloth, torn from Donoven's shirt as he tried desperately to save himself, was wedged between the end of the gigantic rock and the floor of the cave, silent testimony to Donoven's passing.

Harris, next in line behind Donoven, hadn't heard or seen

anything of Donoven's plight. He had been scared half out of his mind after Charlie Scott's death and was in no hurry to follow up too close to Donoven. He had been scanning ahead as he crept along when the piece of shirt in the rock caught his attention immediately.

"H—H—Hey, s—som—somebody get up h—he—here quick and l—l—look at th—this!" he stuttered as he literally shook in his boots. Harris was scared and he didn't care who knew it. The thing he wanted most right now was to be some other place hundreds of miles away. He didn't care where; any place was better than this gloomy hole in the ground that was leading them all to their demise.

O'Neill floated out of the shadows like a phantom suddenly materializing from thin air. "What's the problem?" he asked in a flat, sarcastic voice.

"Th—th—there on the—the g—gr—ground," Harris pointed, now visibly shaken. O'Neill bent over and examined the red blotches.

"Blood," he exclaimed in the same flat voice, but without the sarcasm. Then finally taking hold of the cloth, he gave it a tug. When nothing happened, he pulled harder, but still the piece of shirt would not come loose from its grasp in the rock.

A puzzled look came over his face as he studied the situation at hand. How could a piece of Donoven's shirt become wedged in the stone like this? That Donoven was dead he had no doubt, but where was his body? These questions raced through his mind until, on closer examination, he discovered the hairline crack in the stone floor.

"You three men come here. Three more of you grab their belts and hang on."

Showing them where to stand, he ordered them to place one foot on the other side of the crack and push as hard as they could. At first nothing. Then slowly, ever so slowly the floor began to move downward allowing the piece of shirt to drop out of sight. In the torchlight, the men could see the other end of the stone that made up this part of the cavern floor move upward at the same rate as the stone under foot moved down.

"It was a very clever trap, and Donoven walked right into it," O'Neill said with a ghostly smile on his face. "Very well done, but it will not save them. Everybody backtrack and pay attention," O'Neill snapped.

"What are we looking for, boss?"

O'Neill thought for a moment.

"A narrow path of very smooth stone along one side of the cave. When you find it, yell out, then wait for me."

"Why would there be smooth stone when all the rest is fairly rough?" came a voice from the darkness.

"Because somehow the people who use this cave have to have a way around this trap. My guess is that there is a trail alongside that climbs up the wall and past this area. It will have to be small and narrow or we would have seen it. And it will be worn smooth because of all the concentrated use it gets. Anyone not knowing where it is would lose it in the darkness as we did." O'Neill suddenly realized that, had he tried to find his own way out of the cave instead of following the hostage, he most surely would have fallen prey to the trap as Donoven had done. "Any more questions?"

When no more questions came forth, O'Neill ordered the men to start looking, and within minutes they found what they were looking for. There, just as O'Neill had said, hidden between two boulders, was a narrow path climbing up the side of the wall. From time to time, as the men had moved deeper into the cavern, there had been such boulders scattered about, thereby causing no concern when the men passed these concealing the hidden trail.

"Now we don't stop until we reach the golden city!"

CHAPTER 15

The path was narrow and precarious, at times raising from the main floor of the cave twenty feet or more. Making the men more nervous was the fact that below them, ready to engulf anyone unfortunate enough to slip from the trail, was the gaping mouth of the pit covered only by the thin slab of tilting stone.

One by one the men clung to the wall as they inched their way across to safety. It would have made them feel no less apprehensive to know that the Indians moved along this same unforgiving walkway without hesitation or even a light to guide them by.

After what seemed like hours, they were all safely across and on solid ground again, the only casualties being a few skinned knees and scraped hands. But what overshadowed these minor inconveniences was the small point of light glowing at the end of the tunnel.

"Get those torches out!" O'Neill ordered. "And keep your mouths shut. We'll be lucky if you whimpering jackasses haven't given us away already."

The men hated the insults O'Neill unleashed on them at every opportunity, but not one of them dared risk calling him on them. O'Neill ruled with an iron will, and the men, like the tree to the woodsman's ax, could do nothing to ward off his cutting remarks.

When they had proceeded to within a few hundred yards of

the tunnel opening, O'Neill signaled the men to gather round him so he might give his orders for the imminent raid.

"Now listen carefully," he began. "I don't want any mistakes. When you men chose me as your leader, it was to lead you to the treasure that I had told you about. All I knew was that at the time of the full moon, these people came out from some hidden location carrying large amounts of gold." O'Neill paused to take a long breath. "They used gold idols in some kind of ritual to worship the moon, or some crazy thing like that.

"I really don't know what they worship and I don't care. The point is that I have since found the place where all their gold is stored." O'Neill waited a moment for what he had just said to sink in. When he was sure he had the full attention of the men, he lowered his voice and spoke again. "And that, men, is right here at the end of this cave," he said, pointing at the distant light, a devilish look coming over his face.

"Men, instead of a few saddlebags of gold for each of us, we will have wagon loads!"

At this statement, it was hard for the men to contain themselves, but contain themselves they did, either for fear of being overheard from the outside, or of their boss' vengeance.

"What's the plan, boss?" Ted Tworol asked.

"We simply go in and take the gold by force. Anybody get in our way, we shoot him down. Everybody check your weapons and get ready to go. The hidden valley is just around the bend a few hundred yards."

"What if they don't give up easy?"

"Then we settle in and make camp. That's what I been lugging that tent around for—in case we have to stay awhile. I want to be comfortable for as long as it takes."

The hidden valley spread before them like a picture from the past. Never in all their days had O'Neill's men seen anything like what they now experienced. It was if they had stepped into another world, a land of beauty with none of the harshness of the outside world.

Green grass stretched across a valley of about twenty-five hundred acres, interspersed by long, smooth paths. Along the far side of the valley, where the cliffs seemed to climb right into the clouds, stood a two-story adobe building covered with ornaments of what could only be gold. The reflection in the morning sun was almost blinding.

Scattered in small groups around the building were smaller buildings also of adobe. To the south of these structures there were many livestock corrals filled with goats, pigs, chickens, and to the surprise of the men, peacocks, their tails bristling with color.

O'Neill was quick to point out that the gold was to be found in the two-story building, and it would be their objective to seize the building and remove its contents for their own use.

One thing puzzled O'Neill as he scanned the valley with his field glasses: there was no sign of life. Where were the inhabitants of this mysterious valley before him? Had they all fled in fear of their lives, leaving the treasure to be carried off without a fight? O'Neill pondered these questions for quite awhile as his men waited silently behind him.

Finally, a rooster crowed somewhere in the distance and a goat bleated in answer as if signaling for a time of action.

"Let's go!" O'Neill said abruptly as he stepped out into the light of the new day.

They had walked into the valley for only a few hundred feet when from behind they heard a heavy object crashing into place. When the dust settled, they saw a huge boulder was now blocking the tunnel's entrance, and on a ledge overhead, partially hidden by a stone wall, were ten bronze men armed with the same bows the Indian in the tunnel had carried.

Several guns snapped out of their holsters, and in an instant, bullets began flying toward the would-be ambushers who simply dropped out of sight where the bullets could not reach them.

O'Neill soon realized it was of no use to attack the Indians. They were well hidden from his guns and since the Indians used a ladder to obtain the ledge, then pulled it up after them, there was no way to drive them out of their hiding place.

"Several men cover us with your rifles while we get some distance from that ledge," O'Neill ordered. "Then we'll cover you."

Soon the men were safely out of range and could walk with a little more ease. The village lay a quarter mile to the west and between it and O'Neill's men was a many-layered fountain surrounded by a low wall made of reddish-brown bricks.

As the men got closer, they could hear the water flowing down from one tier of the fountain to the next. At any other time it would have been a pleasant sound, but here and now it blocked all other sounds from reaching the men's ears. And one of those sounds was the movement of warriors crawling up to the other side of the low wall in front of them.

O'Neill was a crafty man, and as he walked, he thought the situation over in his mind. The wall ahead bothered him. Although he saw no movement, he sensed something was not right. Except for the Indians that blocked the tunnel, everything was just too peaceful.

The closer he and his men got to the wall, the more that little voice deep inside told him that it meant danger.

"Everybody stop," O'Neill said at last. "Morgon, bring your pack over here. The rest of you get ready with your rifles."

Taking the pack, O'Neill quickly opened it and withdrew several sticks of dynamite.

"Damn it! I never knew that's what was in that pack when O'Neill told me to carry it," Morgon said to the man beside him. The man looked up and smiled nervously.

"If I'd known, I'd a walked a mite further away from you."

It didn't take long before O'Neill had the dynamite wrapped together and a short fuse protruding from it.

"You men ready?" O'Neill asked as he took a match and put it to the end of the fuse. The men dropped to one knee and brought the rifles up to their shoulders. At the same instant, O'Neill hurled the dynamite over the wall in front of them. It no sooner dropped from sight behind the barrier than a dozen bronze bodies jumped up and took to their heels in a mad scramble to get away from the explosion that was sure to follow.

"Fire!" O'Neill screamed, and the men let loose a barrage of bullets that literally mowed the retreating Indians down before they got ten feet from the wall. When the smoke cleared, all the Indians lay on the ground either dead or wounded.

Suddenly with gun in hand, O'Neill ran forward and dropped over the barricade.

"The dynamite!" someone yelled as O'Neill bent down behind the wall. When O'Neill came to his feet again he had the deadly package in his hand. The fuse was still smoking as he tossed it back toward Morgon, who instinctively caught it before he had time to think about what he was doing.

"No blasting cap," O'Neill laughed as he walked past Morgon, who was still holding the dynamite in trembling hands.

"We'll set up camp by the fountain. One of you men figure a way to shut that damn thing off," O'Neill ordered, jerking his thumb at the fountain. "I don't want to be surprised because we can't hear anything. The rest of you men push those dead Indians over the outer wall and make sure its downwind of us."

One of the men hesitantly came over to O'Neill. "Boss," he said, "some of them Injuns ain't dead yet. What you want done with them?"

"Use your knife and make them dead!" O'Neill ordered.

Lewana watched the killing of her warriors with horror. Her plan had been foolproof, yet instead of O'Neill and his men being her captives, they were now firmly entrenched within rifle shot of her village. She hadn't planned on

O'Neill's use of dynamite to gain the advantage or on his cunning mind.

Since her escape, with the help of the man called Madigan, she knew that O'Neill or someone like him would return to threaten her people. And this was confirmed when two of her most fearsome warriors' bodies were found a few days before, one with his throat cut and his body hidden amongst some rocks by the outside entrance to their valley. The other was shot in the head and left where he fell just inside the hidden valley. She had heard the shot, but her warriors were too late to catch the killer before he escaped.

This new situation called for another plan, one that dare not fail. For to fail a second time would most certainly mean death for her people. Watching O'Neill's men methodically cut the throats of the wounded warriors assured her there would be no mercy if these men captured her village.

She could offer them gold, she thought, for surely that is what they came to steal, but would that be enough? No, there were many beautiful girls in the village and these men would not be satisfied until they had forced their intentions on every one of them.

Lewana shuddered at the thought of these dirty, vulgar men touching the women of her tribe. No, gold would not be enough. She would have to find a way to rid these trespassers from her sacred valley once and for all. And that might require time—time that was fast running out for her and her people.

As Lewana pondered what to do next, a feeling of helplessness came over her. O'Neill, with his superior weapons, was at the one strategic location where he could control the valley around him. With the greater range of his rifles, he could pin down the men on the ledge or in the village while at the same time being out of range of the Indians' arrows.

There was fresh water for them to drink, and depending on their food supply, they could stay for weeks if need be, keeping her people from tending their stock or moving about at all, except on the far side of the village itself, where the buildings gave some protection.

Lewana quickly scanned the ledge over the giant boulder blocking O'Neill's retreat. Those ten men perched up there would last no more than a few days, as there was neither food nor water with them.

That boulder! She would give anything to remove it and hopefully give O'Neill and his men a chance to pull back. At the time it had seemed like a good idea to block the tunnel, not realizing that once the boulder was in place it would be the same as locking yourself in a room with a hungry lion.

Her thoughts went back to the time on the other side of the mountains when the tall man with the quick gun saved her and her friend Mila, and how she had ordered her warriors to find him and protect him from danger if at all possible. She remembered how she hurried to him when one of her warriors returned with the news of his being shot and dying in the old prospector's cabin not far from the hidden valley. She did what she could for him that night with the help of Mila, and when she was called away, he was resting easily.

The next day, when she and Mila returned, they found two more horses in the corral. Fearing for Madigan's life, she sent Mila back to the hidden valley to get help. If Madigan was in danger, she would have her people do what they could.

As night had fallen, Lewana and a warrior crept silently over to the cabin and peered through the window. What they saw gave Lewana much relief, for the two newcomers were obviously friends of the tall man who sat at the table eating with them. She stayed only long enough to make sure he was safe, then left as quietly as she had come, not even giving her presence away to the great horse in the corral. Yet her heart ached, for she might never see him again. That was several days ago.

The sound of gunshots brought Lewana suddenly back to the present. One of the trapped Indians from above the entrance lay sprawled in the dirt at the base of the giant boulder. This brought the number to twenty-seven dead, and there was no end in sight. Something desperately needed to be done.

"Bring me a white flag," Lewana commanded the man next to her. "I must speak to these men before we lose any more of our people.

"But you cannot," the Indian said. "You are our leader. Let one of us go and speak with the evil ones. Your life is too much to risk."

"As your leader, I am the only one who can speak for the people. Is my life worth more than your children's? If I do not find a way to stop this senseless killing, these evil men will not stop until we are all dead."

"But there must be another way," the man protested. "They are many and their food will soon be gone. They will then have to come in close to our village where our arrows will take them in their tracks."

Lewana drew in a deep breath. "And what of our men on the ledge? They have no food or water. They will die soon if we do not get them out of there. No, I see no other way but to talk with them and hope they will take gold and leave."

"And if they will not?" The question came from Mila, who stood slightly behind Lewana. Lewana turned to face her friend. "Then it will be up to you. Come and I will tell you what I want done."

An hour later, Lewana was walking toward O'Neill's stronghold with the white flag above her head. She was frightened, but hid her fear behind a mask of grim determination, for to show fear to these men would bring shame on herself and her people. It might also give O'Neill the confidence to attack the village and Lewana wanted no more of her people to die.

As she moved closer to the fountain, one of O'Neill's men raised a rifle and aimed it in her direction. She braced herself for the bullet only to see the man lower the weapon quickly as O'Neill stepped beside him.

So, O'Neill was interested in hearing her out, she told herself. Then a chilling thought came to her. Did he want to talk . . . or did he want her? She knew in her heart that if he tried to take her, she would find a way to kill him or herself, although she must live long enough for help to arrive, if it was coming. She dared not, could not, believe the tall man would not come if he were able.

Once before, when she was his captive beyond the mountains, she had feared being taken against her will by O'Neill. The only thing preventing it then was the other men he rode with. That they all wanted her and Mila, she knew. The only thing that prevented her and her friend being ravished then were the saddlebags full of gold and the men's fear of being closely pursued by her people.

Still, O'Neill made it very plain what he had in store for her and Mila when they were safely away from the mountains. Luckily, the man called Madigan intervened.

Funny how the air smelled so fresh today, and she couldn't remember when the sky looked so blue or the clouds so white. Was this the day she was to die? Everything depended on Mila now. And on the man with the fast gun.

It was four days since LaRue and Shorty showed up at the cabin. Madigan's wound was healing fast, and most of his strength had returned. All his life Madigan had worked hard and it kept him in top physical condition. Now it was paying off.

This morning Madigan was up early cutting wood for the cook stove from a pile of logs the old prospector must have dragged in for just such a purpose. The night before, LaRue had told Madigan of the old man and the arrow with the golden tip that killed him.

Madigan still had trouble breathing deeply, but with time that would come. It felt good to do some hard work for a change, with being laid up and all. He picked up a bundle of kindling, and took it inside, where he was greeted by the smell of breakfast and hot coffee brewing. Cuttin' wood can make a man mighty hungry, and that bacon sizzling in the skillet made his mouth water. He was startin' to like the idea of eating breakfast.

They had just finished eating when the buckskin snorted a low warning. In an instant the three men grabbed their guns, ready for any threat that might come. What they saw when they looked out the window was an Indian woman accompanied by two warriors.

"Looks like we may be in for an Indian attack," LaRue said as he checked his gun.

"I'm not so sure," Madigan said. "Something about the woman looks familiar. Give me a minute and it'll come to me." Yes, there was something about her, something clawing at the back of his mind. He just couldn't seem to bring it up where he could get a hold of it yet. Must not be in as good a shape as he thought. Ever since he was shot, things were a little confused in his mind.

Madigan's guess was the woman was in her early thirties. She looked to be Indian but with features different than any tribe he'd seen before. That she was a pretty woman, no one could deny. She was tall for an Indian, maybe goin' five-feet-nine or a little taller.

Her skin was dark as an Indian's, yet it was more like white skin tanned from the sun than the reddish skin of the North American Indian, and her hair was more a dark brown than black.

Suddenly it hit Madigan like a poke in the face. She was one of the women he had saved weeks before on the east side of the Rockies. He hadn't recognized her right away because at the time he saved her from the Mexicans, she was dirty, battered, and he thought, shamefully, naked.

Now she was one of the prettiest women he ever did see, and she was just standing out there waiting. Waiting for what, Madigan did not know.

Lewana stepped to the top of the wall without hesitating, then down to the inner circle where O'Neill stood waiting, waiting like a hungry cat for a mouse.

"Well, look who we got here. Couldn't stand to be away from me any longer, huh?" he sneered.

"I have come to talk."

"Talk? Talk! We can talk any time. What I got in mind for you won't take any words. Yes, sir, no words at all," he grinned, lust showing in his eyes. "Soon as the men get the tent up in the morning, you and me are gonna have us a little roll in the sack, among other things," O'Neill said. He would have preferred to vent his lust within the hour, but with the ever present threat of attack, he'd just have to wait till morning.

Lewana was now visibly shaken and she didn't care who saw it. She had walked right into his arms without a fight and she was terrified at the thought of him touching any part of her. She slowly let her hand slide back to a large fold in her flowing blue skirt, feeling for the small dagger concealed there. Unfortunately, one of the men noticed her movements and pointed it out to O'Neill.

Suddenly O'Neill reached over and took the knife from its hiding place. "Gonna use that on me, are you? I ought to cut your throat with it, but I got other ideas for you!" he screamed, throwing the knife away in one swift motion.

"You better use it then!" she blurted in anger and fear. "I'll die before I let you have me!"

She had hardly finished the words before O'Neill's right hand clubbed her alongside her head, knocking her unconscious.

"You don't have much to say about it," he said over her still form. "Somebody get some rope and tie the bitch up. I don't want her running off when I'm ready for her."

This was better than O'Neill could have ever hoped for. Here at his feet was the Indians' leader. Now he felt he had the key to the gold. With Lewana as his hostage, the people would surely lay down their arms and deliver the gold to him anywhere he wished.

What he hadn't reckoned on was the resolve of the girl at his feet. She wasn't chosen their leader for nothing. And she knew the risk she was taking when she started out under the white flag.

When Mila showed up at the little cabin in the hidden canyon, she didn't know what to expect. Lewana had told her what to say once she got the attention of the tall gunman. But one just didn't walk up to a cabin unannounced. A man, or woman for that matter, could get shot. With her limited experience with the white man, Mila had only seen cruelty, except for this man whom she had come to speak with.

The problem was that he was not alone any longer, and for all she knew, he might be laying inside unconscious. If this were the case, how would the others act upon seeing her and the warriors standing in the open?

Her fears melted away when Madigan stepped out from the cabin door and raised his hand in the sign the Indians used for peace. Seeing this man once again reminded her of the time he saved her and Lewana from the outlaws. It seemed so long ago.

This man before her was tall, with broad shoulders and narrow hips. His gray eyes always seemed somewhat amused, except, she thought, when he was forced to kill. Then she remembered how they had suddenly gone cold and seemed to pierce right through her.

His hair was light brown, almost blond, and was cut short and well-trimmed compared to other cowboys she'd seen, certainly much shorter than most Indians wore their hair. His face was an honest face with strong, yet somehow gentle features. He was well muscled and there was a confidence about him she could not remember seeing in any other man. If anyone was able to help her people, it would be this man.

She was happy to see he moved with an ease and grace not often seen in big men. It also showed his wound was healing fast. The gun hung low on his hip did not escape her notice either.

After hearing Mila's story and giving her and her two friends food and drink, LaRue, Shorty, and Madigan made quick plans to follow Mila back to the hidden valley.

Mila told them that they were the first white men to ever enter the valley by invitation, and Madigan wished it weren't for the job at hand. She also said the leader of the outlaws was none other than Harry O'Neill.

At O'Neill's name, Shorty suddenly remarked, "I should have killed that maggot back when I had the chance!" About now, they all wished he had. No one needed to tell them O'Neill was a violent and vicious man, one who'd stop at nothing to get what he wanted, even if it took killing every man, woman, and child in his way.

Seeing Mila again and remembering how Lewana affected him with her even greater beauty made Madigan's task at hand more urgent. They all knew that O'Neill might kill the men and children at the drop of a hat, but the women would be another matter altogether.

O'Neill was a convicted rapist. Now given the freedom to do whatever he wanted, he would make it a living hell for any woman he wanted.

Madigan's blood ran cold with the thought of Lewana falling prey to O'Neill's evil desires.

CHAPTER 16

By the time they all saddled up, the sun was almost down, leaving growing shadows in its wake. In a strange sort of way, Madigan felt good about finally having a showdown with O'Neill, and he suspected LaRue and Shorty felt the same.

Each of them had his own reasons for wanting to be done with this troublesome rogue that had hurt so many, and as they rode out it was as if three knights in shining armor were going off to the Crusades. But there would be no glory in what they intended to do, only death.

As they rode, Madigan held his Winchester across his lap while the Sharps filled the rifle boot. He was glad to have replaced the lever bolt with a spare one LaRue had given him. Before leaving, he had made sure there was ample ammunition for both.

"You think you'll need that?" LaRue asked, nodding toward the Sharps as he prodded his horse up alongside Madigan.

"Hope not, but I've always kind've liked the gun, and we may need the range, from what Mila tells us. If O'Neill's holed up at any distance, the Sharps might give us the edge we need."

"See what you mean. But are you up to firing that thing? I shot one of them once, and it almost knocked me on my butt," LaRue said, grinning at the experience he remembered.

It was a good question and one Madigan had asked himself several times since riding out. "I won't know the answer to that until I've pulled the trigger," he answered. "If we're lucky, we won't have to find out." Still, Madigan wondered about it himself. His wound was healing fast, but it would be some time before he felt like his old self again.

As they rode along, Mila told them about the cave that was the entrance to the hidden valley. She also told the men of its dangers to the uninitiated. But as she explained later, they would not have to worry about the tunnel or its traps, for they would get into the valley as she and her comrades had come out.

Upon questioning her further, she explained, "We waited until Lewana had the attention of O'Neill and his men, then we slipped quickly up a narrow foot trail to the top of the rim. From there, we followed the trail across the top of the rim some five hundred yards to the outer edge where it dropped down the side of the rock face to a ledge a hundred feet above the outer floor.

"Lowering a rope ladder, which was kept there for such a purpose, we climbed down the rest of the way and walked to the cabin."

Lewana had placed herself in grave peril to try to save her people. And at the thought of O'Neill touching her, a rage came up within Madigan that turned his blood cold. Then just as suddenly, he came to the realization that he was in love with Lewana! He had only met her twice, but it was enough.

He'd heard of people falling in love at first sight but didn't think it possible. Never had it occurred to Madigan he could be in love with her, or anyone for that matter.

But it was true! Since their first meeting he often thought of her and it always gave him a warm feeling inside. But love her! It had taken the thought of her in another man's arms to make Madigan see the truth. Now more than ever, he had to save her or die trying!

By the time they arrived at the spot where they would make camp, it was well after dark, and although Madigan wanted desperately to go on, there was nothing more they could do until daylight. It would be impossible to follow the ledge up the side of the cliff with no light to see by. They built a small fire, and unrolled their bedrolls out in the shadows at the base of the cliff.

Only men new to the West ever slept close to the fire. The firelight not only blinded those too close to it, but also let anyone coming up on the camp see without being seen.

Morning came with the first gray dawn breaking into the blazing light of the desert sun. By the time the rocks began to warm, they were already high on the cliff above their camp carrying their packs along a narrow trail cut into the side of the shear wall.

As he walked along, Madigan noticed that in places the trail was cut out of the solid stone face of the cliff. Yet weathered as it was, it seemed like it had been done by nature.

"How did your people find this trail?"

Mila smiled as though reading Madigan's thoughts. "You mean how old is this trail, don't you? My people cut this and several more over four hundred years ago, when they first came to the hidden valley.

"They were running from the Spaniards that came and destroyed our people's homes many miles to the south of here. Our people were very rich with gold and jewels, and the Spanish wanted all the wealth for themselves.

"The people tried at first to fight them, but more and more Spanish came from the sea. We had many warriors in those days, numbering into the many thousands, whereas the Spanish had only a few hundred at first.

"Yet, the Spanish wore armor and used cannons and guns. We used only clubs and swords made of wood. Many of our people would die at each attack while only wounding a few of the Spanish, and the fighting went on for many days.

"Finally, when our leader saw that it was useless to fight, he tried to reason with the Spanish. For a while it worked, but then the priest stirred up the people. Our leader was killed by one of our own warriors as he stood on a porch beside the Spanish leader.

"The priest said it was a mistake, that the warrior who shot the arrow was trying to kill the Spanish general. We knew he lied. So in the night, several thousand of our people took what gold they could carry and started to the north after burying all the rest of the gold and jewels they could lay their hands on."

"You mean the Spanish hadn't gotten all the gold yet?" LaRue asked.

"No, they thought they had most of it, but they were only in possession of a small portion. Most of the gold and jewels was hidden when the first Spanish ship was sighted in the bay. It was the keepers of this treasure that were the forebearers of us in the valley.

"There had been a prophecy that foretold of the coming of the Spanish, so our people prepared themselves accordingly. It is the gold they brought here to the valley that O'Neill is after, and we will give it to him to save our Queen's life, if that's what it takes."

So the truth was out. Lewana was not only their leader, she was their queen! Madigan felt himself go sick in the stomach. The woman he was in love with was a queen, and for all Madigan knew about queens, she would not be allowed to marry a commoner.

And, Madigan reflected, that was exactly what he was to these people—a commoner, and not even of her own blood. Yet, this knowledge did not alter the fact that he was deeply in love with Lewana and that she was in danger.

Soon they were at the top of the cliff, the climb taking the better part of an hour, with the heavy packs they all carried on their backs. As Madigan looked to the east, he was blinded by the sun just barely creeping over the rim of the plateau. If they hurried, they could get to a position on the east side of the rim and be able to scout the valley below with the sun at their backs. They would have to plan on just the right moment so that the sun blinded the men below.

Madigan's first plan of action was to get the men on the ledge up to safety, and to this end he had the rope ladder carried to the top with them. He'd figured they'd better move fast as the sun climbed rapidly in the morning sky, and much would depend on the outlaws not being able to see the warriors climb up the ladder to safety.

Madigan's first sight of the hidden valley was one of awe. They were lying on their stomachs at the edge of the rim with the sun behind them, below was the ledge on which the Indians were trapped, and beyond was the fountain with O'Neill's camp spread around it.

Beyond that was the village of white buildings standing brilliant in the first rays of the morning sun. One building stood out from the rest, and this, Mila told Madigan, was the repository of the treasure of her ancestors. This building was much larger than all the others and on its walls hung great disks of gleaming gold.

Glancing over his shoulder, he motioned the man with the rope ladder forward. "We must hurry to get the stranded men off the ledge before the sun climbs much higher and gives away our protective shield of light," Madigan whispered to him.

In a matter of seconds they tied the ladder to a huge rock and lowered the other end to the ledge below. Quickly the Indian climbed down to the ledge to inform those below what was at hand and to help any man too weak to make it by himself.

Thinking of the terrible thirst these men must have endured, Madigan sent a second Indian down with several canteens of water. Soon the trapped men started the climb up to freedom.

Madigan was so intent on getting the men off the ledge that he hadn't taken time to scout for signs of Lewana. As the last man came up over the edge, the ladder was quickly pulled up after him so as to leave no evidence of the rescue. No need to alert O'Neill to their presence before they were ready, Madigan thought.

Carefully moving into the shadow of the boulder, Madigan

raised his field glasses and took a good look around. To his shock, he saw Lewana lying on the ground by the fountain. His heart leaped with the sight of her lying there, quickly followed by anger at the men who held her prisoner.

Lewana and Madigan were separated by only a few hundred yards, yet it might as well have been miles, for all the help he could give her. He couldn't even tell if she was dead or alive.

Lewana lay where she had fallen. The morning sun beat hot on her back but she did not move, for to do so would give away the fact that she was no longer unconscious. Her hands and feet were bound and she could not tell whether she was being watched. She was surprised to find that she had been unconscious all night.

Somewhere behind her she heard the sound of men working, the sound of heavy canvas being dragged along the ground. Was even now O'Neill standing over her waiting for her to come around?

Overhead an eagle soared in ever-widening circles, a silent bystander to the drama below. A warm breeze blew gently through her hair, bringing with it the odor of half a dozen men soiled from days in the saddle.

Her hands ached from being tied behind her back and she was stiff from lying still, yet her mind was alert, searching for any possible way to escape. Was the tall man out there close by, ready to help when the opportunity presented itself? It did not occur to Lewana that he might not come. She only knew that he must come, for her people's very lives depended on him and she could not believe anything else.

Behind her a man coughed and footsteps came closer.

"I seen you with your eyes open," a voice said. "Maybe you can use some water. Don't worry about O'Neill seeing you drink. He's still in his blankets. It'll be our little secret."

The thin man squatted down beside her and rolled her gently on her side. Holding her head so she could drink, he offered the tin cup up to her lips. The water tasted cool as it trickled down her dry throat and she drank slowly so as not to waste any. She was in mid-swallow when to her shock she felt his hand slide down the front of her shirt and take hold of her breast. She tried to roll away, but he dropped the tin cup in the dirt and grabbed her with his free hand.

Terrified, she started to scream, then a thought struck her. "If you don't get away from me and stay away, I'll tell O'Neill what you are doing, and that you told me you plan to kill him when his back is turned so you can have me for yourself!"

The man's hand froze. "What makes you think he'll believe you?"

The man was right, but Lewana had no choice but to go on with the bluff. "Maybe he won't." She raised her eyes to meet his. "But shall we find out?" she said defiantly.

"Look, ma'am, I didn't mean you no harm," he said as he withdrew his hand. "I don't know what got into me. You being such a pretty woman and all, I just lost my head for a moment, that's all. You got to believe me! I didn't mean you no harm, honest!"

Lewana was about to demand him to leave when she got another idea. "I'll make a deal with you," she began. "You bring me some more water whenever you can without O'Neill seeing you, and I'll keep quiet about what happened. If I get thirsty, I tell everything. Understand?"

The thin man looked away from her. "Understood," he replied. "I'll bring you more water now before O'Neill gets out of the sack," he said as he came to his feet and walked off.

The thin man remembered vividly the fate of Warren Elegant, and knew full well he'd receive the same if O'Neill even thought he was trying to pull something behind his back.

For the moment Lewana was safe, but there was no way of telling what would happen when O'Neill got up.

Looking over the scene before him very carefully, Madigan assessed the situation. Lewana was held captive directly in front of him. To his right was the entrance to the tunnel that was now blocked by a boulder, keeping O'Neill, his men, and the Indians trapped also.

To Madigan's left stood the Indian village. Encircling this valley were shear rock cliffs, and Madigan and his friends were on top of those cliffs.

Any animal is more dangerous when trapped, and O'Neill was no exception. So the first thing to be done was give O'Neill an escape route, and that meant removing the boulder from the cave's mouth. They had enough blasting powder to do the job; only trouble was, if they set the charge inside the cave, it might bring down the roof.

There was only one thing to do and that was to set the charge in such a way as to roll the rock to the side. Of course, it was easier said than done. Someone would have to crawl under the edge of the boulder and place the charge just right. And they had no way of knowing if there was even room for a man to get it under the boulder. A further problem was the fact that if there was room enough, it might expose the person to rifle fire. A bullet didn't take much room to kill.

After talking it over with LaRue and Shorty, it was decided that Shorty would have the best chance of pulling it off. LaRue and Madigan were just too darn big for the job, but it didn't make either of them feel any better about having to send their friend to do the dangerous work.

"We'll keep them so occupied they won't even know you're around!" LaRue promised. For Madigan's part, it was the first time in his life he'd wished he weren't so damn large.

Madigan gave Shorty enough fuse so he'd have at least three minutes to get out once he struck a match to it, then took an old axle grease can, wiped it clean so it wouldn't foul the powder, and packed it to the brim with blasting powder.

After packing it, he secured the lip and punched a hole just large enough for the fuse and wrapped the whole affair with rope to make it into the neatest little bomb you ever saw.

Soon Shorty was on his way down the outer wall with Mila and one of the warriors leading the way. They figured it'd take three hours before Shorty could get to the inside of the boulder, so Madigan and LaRue sat down to wait, each of them lost in his own thoughts. The biggest one on Madigan's mind was whether he would be able to save Lewana in time.

Several times he checked on Lewana, his heart aching at the thought of her lying there, possibly hurt. Oh, how he wanted to lay waste to the men that held her captive.

"You think Shorty will be able to get the can far enough under the rock to move it out of the way?" LaRue asked after a while.

Madigan picked up his binoculars and took a long, hard look at the boulder below.

"From what I can see from here, there seems to be a little room under the north end of it. Might just be room to get the charge in the right place. If we're lucky," he added.

The hours dragged on slowly, and Madigan wanted desperately to know how Lewana was doing. He would have given anything to speed the time up.

He was just taking a slow drink of water, letting it trickle down his throat, when movement from below caught Madigan's eye. Rolling out of his blankets was the unmistakable image of Harry O'Neill, his snowy white hair standing out like a beacon in the night.

A fleeting thought ran through Madigan's mind upon seeing him. Just one shot and O'Neill would be no more, just a hunk of dead flesh rotting in the sun, meat for the vultures to feast on. Nothing more, nothing less.

LaRue must have read Madigan's mind at that very moment. "We can't take a chance on killing O'Neill yet. No telling what his men might do. If they rush the village, the Indians won't have a chance.

"Unless he tries something, we have to wait it out. Maybe when the boulder's out of the way, they'll fall back, and we can keep them pinned down long enough for the Indians to get her out of there."

"I guess you're right," Madigan said reluctantly, while mentally calculating the distance he'd have to hold over to make a one-shot kill on O'Neill.

The Indians, with Shorty following close behind, moved swiftly through the cave, arriving at the boulder fifteen minutes earlier than planned. Shorty wasted no time making preparations for what he had to do. From where they stood, they could plainly see light showing around parts of the huge rock.

Upon closer examination, Shorty found what he needed— just enough room to slide the explosive into place. It would be a tight squeeze with little room to spare, but by lying down and pushing the charge ahead of him he could do it. Getting down on his stomach, he carefully pushed the package into place and left the fuse to trail back behind him.

He still had his hands on the canister when a shadow fell across the opening. If he were discovered now there would be no chance for escape and he knew it. He held his breath and waited, time standing still, the air hot and dry.

Then he heard it, the unmistakable caw of a crow. It was nothing more than a crow landing outside, blocking the light. Still, if the crow sensed his presence, he might give warning and make known Shorty's whereabouts. One rifle bullet and Shorty would be blown to bits along with the Indians in back of him.

Funny how he had always liked the birds, their black bodies glistening in the sun, their caws echoing in the morning's still air like an angry wife scolding her husband for some wrongdoing, imagined or real. He'd always liked that sound. Now it might very well mean his death.

Shorty lay absolutely still, breathing through his mouth to prevent getting a whiff of dust in his nose causing a sneeze. After what seemed like hours, the crow took flight, and Shorty relaxed his tense and aching muscles.

He was just starting to pull back when his eye caught movement. He froze, not knowing what to expect. When his eyes adjusted, he was terrified by what he saw. There, not a foot away from his face, moving out of the hot morning sun, was the largest rattler he'd ever seen. If the snake struck, there would be no hope in avoiding its fangs and the certain and agonizing death that was to follow.

Sweat ran down Shorty's forehead and into his eyes, making him want to blink, but he dare not blink no matter how much his eyes burned. Maybe, just maybe, the snake would find it too cool in the cave, move out, and look for a more comfortable place to spend the day. Shorty prayed.

Perspiration soaked his shirt as the snake moved an inch closer before stopping to test the air with its flickering tongue, the four-inch-wide head hovering just above the ground, dead eyes looking into Shorty's like the demon of hell itself. In his heart, Shorty was suddenly aware he was about to die.

CHAPTER 17

The serpent's head swayed slightly back and forth while the rest of its thick, muscular body slowly coiled around to the striking position. Shorty braced for the fangs to sink into his flesh, but no matter what, he thought, before I die I will light the fuse, if it takes my dying breath.

The rattler drew back as if finally aware of Shorty, its tail starting to buzz its deadly warning. Shorty closed his eyes and waited for the strike that within seconds would come, sweat beading on his forehead, his breath coming short and shallow. The snake tensed pulling its head back before the strike.

Shorty heard the rush of air as the snake's head flew by his right ear. Now the fangs would find their mark, releasing a lethal dose of venom. But there was no pain, no feeling at all! Had the snake missed? More likely, it had aimed for his neck and even now was sinking its fangs in deeply.

Shorty had talked to men who had been snake bitten and lived. They told him of the instant of the hit and how they didn't for the first few seconds realize they were even bitten. Then after the venom flowed deep into the muscle, a white, hot pain would radiate outward from the wound and finally the arm or leg would go numb.

He remembered hearing one old prospector say, "If a man's in good health and the snake's not too big, the poison will just make you durn sick, but you'll live. Course'n that's if the snake's a small one and he only gets you in an arm or leg and not too high at that.

"If a man gets careless and puts his head down a hole and gets a snake bite, then it's all over, but the buryin'."

The thought of white, hot pain kept going through Shorty's mind. But he still felt no pain, nothing, not even a little sting. He opened his eyes slowly and to his great shock, the serpent's head was pinned squarely to the dirt, an arrow stuck between its eyes, its body writhing in the last death throes.

Madigan half-dozed off in the morning heat, his head dropping to his chest before he caught himself. He glanced around quickly to see if LaRue noticed.

"What's the time?" he asked. LaRue was the only one of them that carried a pocket watch.

"It's been about three hours since Shorty left. Suppose we better get ready so he can start the fireworks show below?" LaRue asked.

"You're probably right. How do you want to handle this?"

"Just pick an easy target and start shooting, I guess. I wish there were another way, but we've got no choice." LaRue hesitated. "Let's give it another five minutes to make sure Shorty's in position," he suggested. Madigan nodded in agreement.

"Maybe O'Neill will be an easy target then," Madigan hissed under his breath, relishing the thought of putting a bullet in his enemy.

After O'Neill got up from his blankets, things got pretty quiet around the camp. He only glanced in the direction of Lewana once, then found himself a comfortable place in the shade of the fountain, and sat back to drink coffee and light a cigar that he puffed on occasionally, although not enough to keep it lit.

What was on his mind, Madigan wondered. Lewana? Or

was he trying to figure a way out of the mess he'd gotten into? O'Neill was a rogue and a mean one at that, but as much as Madigan hated to admit it, he was also a thinker when things got rough.

Something was keeping O'Neill preoccupied, and whatever it was, Madigan knew it wasn't good. He kept watching O'Neill sitting there in the shade while Lewana was now fully exposed to the sun, and the anger started up in Madigan's throat again. He made up his mind that no matter what, he was going to nail O'Neill on the spot if he made the slightest move toward her.

Sitting there watching the man below made the time go even slower, and Madigan was just about to ask LaRue how long they had left when a white puff of smoke caught Madigan's eye.

"She's going to blow!" he yelled as he brought his Sharps up to his shoulder.

With a violent explosion, the rock blocking the entrance to the tunnel shuddered once, then almost in slow motion rolled a few feet to the side. Not much, but enough to allow one man at a time to pass into the cave.

Immediately, O'Neill was on his feet and running. Madigan fired a shot in O'Neill's direction but missed clean. Below was pandemonium, and adding to the confusion, was a large dust cloud thrown up by the blast. It now obscured their vision of what was happening below.

Madigan hastily broke the breech open on the Sharps and replaced the spent round with a good one. He needn't have been in a hurry, for below them nothing could be seen except a giant dust cloud roiling up from the canyon floor like a storm gone mad. LaRue looked over at Madigan and shrugged his shoulders.

There was nothing for them to do but wait for the dust to settle and pray Lewana would still be all right. At least the air was fairly calm in the valley so they wouldn't have to wait long.

"Fire a couple of rounds in the air to keep them moving. No use letting them get too settled!" Madigan yelled.

"I'd like to blast away into the valley only I'd be afraid of hitting the girl!" LaRue yelled back as he fired off a couple of rounds from his Winchester.

What seemed like hours, but really was only minutes, passed and the dust settled to the point where they could see again. When it cleared sufficiently, Madigan took careful aim at a man standing in the open and pulled the trigger.

"That's one we won't have to worry about," LaRue said as the man hit the ground.

"You might say that," Madigan answered grimly as he jacked another round in the Sharps. Madigan could tell by LaRue's tone of voice that he was feeling the same as he was about what they were forced to do. No true Western man likes to kill, and to kill this way, like shooting prairie dogs on the north range, was something that nagged at Madigan's stomach.

Yet they had no choice. These men wanted the Indians' gold and didn't mind killing for it. And before they killed, they would rape the women and torture the men and boys. These men gave no mercy and deserved none in return.

Madigan was about to find another target when a barrage of bullets swept over the rim of the canyon at them, ricocheting off the boulders around them like deadly lead hornets. For the better part of ten minutes the outlaws kept up the bombardment. When things had settled down so Madigan could take a look again, he was sick at what he saw. Lewana was gone!

Madigan quickly looked for O'Neill, but the madman was nowhere to be found. His heart sank in a pool of despair as he realized O'Neill had made his escape and taken Lewana with him, and there was only one place they could have gone— into the tunnel to try to make it to the outside.

When Madigan had first realized that the rock blocking the tunnel had to be removed, his plans were for Shorty and the Indians to set the bomb in place, light the fuse, and run like the dickens to get out of the tunnel before O'Neill's men might get close enough to get a shot at them. Madigan had given Shorty enough fuse to burn three minutes.

But what if Shorty decided to stop for some reason? He would be able to hear someone coming behind in the dark but wouldn't know that Lewana was with O'Neill as his hostage, and she might be killed by mistake.

Madigan said a silent prayer, one of the few he'd said in his life, for her safety. He wanted to go as fast as he could to her rescue and started to get up to leave when LaRue's voice stopped him cold.

"Madigan! I know what you've got in mind, but don't do it! Lewana put herself on the line for her people to give them time for you to get here. Now, for Lewana's sake, help me drive her enemies out of the valley!

"Once they're in the tunnel, the villagers can roll the rock back in place. Then we'll go after O'Neill. And if he's hurt the girl in any way, I swear I'll drag him back and let the Indians have him. I promise you that! And from what I hear, they know how to kill a man slowly so he begs to die."

With as much anger as Madigan carried inside, he didn't want to listen to anyone, but LaRue made sense, and Madigan knew in his heart that LaRue was right. He settled back for the job at hand.

Most of the men below were well hidden behind the fountain or low wall that surrounded it. Once in a while a head would pop out as if testing to see if the men above were still there. Madigan and LaRue both held their fire, waiting for a target they couldn't miss. Madigan's shoulder was bothering him some and he didn't want to aggravate the wound any more than he needed to.

The trouble was, the longer they waited, the more time O'Neill had to get away, and the less chance Madigan would see Lewana alive again. Something would have to be done, and done quick.

"I'm going to hike over to the far side of the rim," he told LaRue. "With the Sharps, I might be able to drive them out of hiding. It'll be up to you to keep them moving in the right direction.

"Any of them head for the tunnel, let 'em go. If they try for the village, we'll have to stop them or we'll have a slaughter on our hands."

Madigan didn't wait for LaRue to answer. He grabbed his gear and was up and moving at a fast walk for the other side of the canyon rim. He'd have to stay well back from the inner edge so as to not give his position away before he was ready.

At least this end of the canyon was narrower than at the village end and wouldn't take long to get around. In ten minutes of pushing himself, Madigan was settled in place.

His heart beat so hard it felt like it was coming out of his chest, so Madigan made himself breathe deeply until his body became calm again. Couldn't afford to miss any shots. He noticed the wound was bleeding through his shirt again and it hurt like hell, but pain was something a man can block from his mind if he needs to bad enough.

Carefully edging up until he could just barely see the fountain area below, he checked the wind, figured the distance, and brought the heavy buffalo gun up to his shoulders, all in one deliberate motion.

Almost by itself, the gun slammed against Madigan's shoulder. When the smoke cleared, another man lay dead in the hot sun. The others were scattering in all directions.

Two of O'Neill's men made the mistake of running toward the village. LaRue dropped them in their tracks before they went twenty feet. Pretty good shooting, Madigan thought as he squeezed off another round at a cowboy that was too confused to go anywhere. The man dropped with a thud, then started to get up, fell back down, and lay still.

They'd whittled O'Neill's men down some, but there was still enough left to do some real harm if they didn't get them out of the hidden valley soon. This wasn't a game, and things could get desperate in a hurry if anything went wrong, like LaRue or Madigan catching a stray bullet.

Two things bothered Madigan. The first and foremost was the thought of O'Neill taking Lewana further away from him each minute he was forced to stay here. The second was the fact that it wouldn't stay daylight forever. Once it got dark they would have no way of keeping O'Neill's men under their guns.

They might choose to head for the escape route that lay open to them, or they might choose to go into the village for the gold and maybe a few hostages. Something needed to be done in a hurry, only Madigan didn't know what. At least for the moment the men were making themselves scarce.

Using the momentary lag in activity, Madigan picked up his binoculars and carefully scanned the fountain area. There had to be something he could use to his advantage.

In the army he was taught to always take the high ground wherever possible, then scout the enemy's camp for anything you could use against them. It can be something small, going unnoticed to the casual eye, yet to the trained soldier it might be used as a weapon to bring the enemy to defeat.

Madigan was hoping for something now, only he didn't know what. Only desperation told him there had to be some tool for him to use if he could just find it. He must've glassed the camp several times before giving up. There just wasn't anything he could use to an advantage.

The men were well hidden, and with the fountain standing close to the wall, it was possible for them to keep out of sight from LaRue and Madigan at the same time. They'd have to move their own positions in order to find a target below. The outlaws weren't likely to show themselves again if they didn't have to.

The mind acts in strange and mysterious ways, so the saying goes. You try to solve a problem, and not finding an answer, you finally give up. But your subconscious goes right on working at it. Then when you least expect it, out pops the answer you were looking for.

So it was now. Madigan had been looking over the outlaws' camp, finding nothing but a half-raised tent and a pile of supplies. Each man carried his own guns so there was no weapons stack. Spread here and there a few bedrolls were laid out. Just inside the west wall another couple of small packages sat off by themselves.

Suddenly it hit him. Mila said O'Neill tossed dynamite at the Indians to scare them off. That was it! Those packs must hold the dynamite! Remembering back to the army, Madigan realized O'Neill always carried explosives with him in a pack like the ones he now concentrated on. Hopefully, this was the solution Madigan was looking for.

While many a man can face the thought of being shot, few can face being blown to bits. Madigan was betting these men weren't any different. Madigan formed a quick plan in his mind and hoped LaRue was ready to keep them going in the right direction once he put his plan in action.

When a big bullet hits the dirt, it throws up a lot of dust. The Sharps was a large gun that shot a big bullet. Taking careful aim, Madigan let fly a shot just short of the packs he hoped carried the explosives. Madigan knew LaRue was wondering what he was up to, but it didn't matter if he knew or not. It was the results Madigan was after.

Sure enough, when the bullet kicked up dirt a few feet from the first pack, every man down there took notice. A few men quickly changed positions, in the process exposing their flanks to LaRue. But LaRue held his fire as Madigan hoped he would. A second shot, this time a little closer to the packs, brought a definite response. The rest of the men put anything they could between themselves and the explosives.

Madigan waited and watched while the outlaws fidgeted at any noise around them. One man coughed, and they all jerked their heads down. It was plain to see they expected the worst. Often the anticipation is harder on one's nerves than the event itself. Like dropping one boot and not the other, he'd gotten their attention. Now they were beginning to crack.

A third shot got the men up and running. Those that ran the wrong way either dropped from LaRue's rifle fire or turned tail and ran the right way. A few more shots from Madigan's Sharps kept the slow ones moving. In a few seconds they managed to herd all the men through the narrow hole that led to the interior of the tunnel.

With a sigh of relief, Madigan leaned back against a rock. His wound had gotten worse and the pain was fierce, yet he felt good at his accomplishment. Now he had to gather his breath and get after O'Neill, but first there was one more thing he had to do.

In less than half an hour, Madigan had set the packs of explosives just inside the tunnel mouth and had lit the fuses after first firing a couple of rounds into the darkness to be sure the outlaws were well back. It wasn't so much that he wanted them safe from the explosion as much as he didn't want to get a bullet in his back while he was leaving.

He knew the tunnel walls were fairly smooth for several hundred yards inside and his bullets would ricochet everywhere. Only an idiot would be foolhardy enough to stick around with lead bouncing all over the place.

He'd given himself enough fuse to get back up on the rim to safety before the charge went off. Madigan's timing was perfect. Just as he got back in position beside LaRue, the whole thing blew with an ear-splitting roar that shook the ground like an earthquake.

When the smoke and dust cleared, they could see that the tunnel was sealed at this end for all eternity. This done, Madigan was now free to find O'Neill. He only prayed Lewana was still alive.

After lighting the fuse, Shorty and the others headed out of the tunnel at a run. Not having any experience with blasting powder, Shorty wanted to put as much ground between himself and the bomb. After crossing over the ledge that bypassed the tilting slab of stone, Mila motioned for the party to take a rest among a jumble of boulders. It was here Shorty got an idea.

When O'Neill and his men came out, they too would have to use the ledge over the tilt stone. At that time they would be very susceptible to an ambush. And if Shorty had his way, he would make sure they got one. Quickly outlining his plan to Mila and the rest, he sat down with them to wait. It was after the first explosion that they heard someone coming.

"Looks like we have company," Shorty said quietly. "Now, everybody get ready. When they hit the ledge, we can pick them off one by one if they want to make a fight of it. Then again, if they'll give up and drop their guns, that's all right with me. We'll take O'Neill back for trial and you and your people can have the rest. I'm sure you'll want an accounting from them for your people they killed."

Mila had a strain to her voice when she spoke. "If they have harmed Lewana in any way, we will make them pay very slowly for their evil!"

No one needed to tell Shorty what pay slowly meant. Mila's people were descended from the Aztecs, and they knew how to make an enemy suffer for his sins.

As the bobbing torch came closer, Shorty was able to see only two people: the unmistakable form of Harry O'Neill, and the slim figure of Lewana.

"What do we do now?" Mila whispered in the darkness.

"We wait and see. If O'Neill drops his guard, we nail him to the wall, but only if we are sure Lewana will be safe. If not, we let them pass and hope Madigan can catch O'Neill before he hurts her."

"I don't like letting him get away, but we may have no choice."

"May be the only chance Lewana has. O'Neill will want to put as much ground between him and Madigan as he can, as fast as he can."

"He might kill Lewana first," worried Mila.

Shorty took her hand in his and squeezed it gently. "I doubt it. O'Neill wants the gold mighty bad. Anybody else would have used Lewana as a trade. Not O'Neill. He wants both. Now he has her and he won't rest until he has the gold too. Madigan knows that and he'll stop O'Neill one way or another. You can bet on it."

When they reached the ledge, O'Neill placed his torch in a crack in the rock and ordered Lewana to light another, all the time keeping a gun pressed at her back. Then he forced her to carry the second torch while they crossed the ledge. "Just in case you drop the light," he had told her, "I don't want to be left in the dark."

Never once did he let the cocked gun move away from her body, leaving Shorty not the slightest chance of a shot at O'Neill without risking Lewana's life. In quiet frustration, he was left with no choice but to let O'Neill slip on by. But for those that followed, it would be another story.

Now that there were no longer any hostages to get in the way, they would be waiting for the rest of the outlaws and Shorty was determined to let no one else escape.

"When they come, I'll confront them at the ledge. Those that want to surrender can. Those that want to make a fight of it . . . well, I'll be ready," Shorty said dryly.

It felt good to have the buckskin under him again. When Madigan got to the outside entrance to the tunnel, it was plain to see by the tracks that O'Neill was gone. There in the dust was the imprint of his heavy boot, beside it the small moccasin tracks of a girl. Madigan was surprised to find no sign of Shorty and Mila.

There was no time to lose. He would worry about them later after he caught up with O'Neill. Anything could happen out here in the high desert country. O'Neill was a desperate and crafty man, and he wouldn't leave any more of a trail than a mountain lion over rock. The slightest breeze would erase all traces of his passing, leaving Madigan with only a guess as to where O'Neill went, and taking away all hope for Lewana's safety at the same time.

Judging from the sign, O'Neill was in a big hurry to get away. He was taking long strides, half dragging Lewana after him. Every once in a while he stopped, probably to get a better hold on the girl, then off he went again, still dragging her.

A short distance more and Madigan came to a place where horses were tied. The tracks on the ground showed where two horses were led away from the rest. He couldn't tell for sure, but it looked as though O'Neill had stopped and possibly tied Lewana's hands before they mounted up and rode off. The memory came back to Madigan of how the outlaws had tied Lewana's and Mila's hands before, and a rage started up within him again.

He'd ridden an hour when he heard the sound of a rider approaching from back down the trail. Madigan reined the buckskin up a dry creek bed where he could see without being seen. It was Shorty.

"Hold up down there!" Madigan yelled when Shorty came into view.

Shorty brought his horse to a halt and waited for Madigan to ride up beside him. "The others won't be bothering anybody again," he said grimly.

"How's that?"

"We waited for them to gain the ledge over the tilt stone after letting O'Neill go by. No way of stopping him without hurting Lewana. When they were all on the ledge, I ordered them to throw down their guns. They answered with a shower of lead instead. Lucky to get under cover before I was killed!

"I was getting ready to pick a few of them off when all of a sudden I hear this ear-rending commotion coming from the area of the tilt stone. Next thing I know, the tilt stone along with the ledge the men were on dropped out of sight. Seems the Indians had the whole thing rigged in case they needed it in an emergency. There wasn't one chance in a million any of 'em survived.

"The Indians won that battle for us. Now it is up to you and me to get Lewana back if we can.

"By the way, LaRue said he'd try to catch up with us as soon as he can. Mila asked him to blow the outside entrance to the tunnel up so it can't be used again. I'd have done it, but just blowing that boulder out of the way scared the stuffings out of me. Of course, the snake didn't help either!"

"What snake?" Madigan asked.

"I'd just gotten the charge in place when this big snake comes . . ."

Shorty was suddenly thrown to the ground as his horse was shot out from under him. One second he was telling Madigan about a snake, the next he was on the ground with the wind knocked out of him.

For an instant Madigan watched as Shorty lay where he had fallen trying to get some air back into his lungs. There was nothing Madigan could do for him. Suddenly a second bullet whistled past Madigan's ear. Madigan's mind blew into a rage. He jerked the buckskin around and headed in the direction of the shot. In the middle of the trail, smoking rifle in hand, stood the killer, Harry O'Neill.

O'Neill levered another round into the chamber. Madigan saw the puff of smoke and felt a tug at his hips, but the great horse beneath him charged on straight at the killer as Madigan's right hand dropped to his Colt. He had no conscious thought of firing his gun, but as he bore down on O'Neill the outlaw began to take on a strange, contorted look. One after another, Madigan saw splotches of red explode on O'Neill's chest. Then another puff of smoke came from O'Neill's rifle and Madigan felt the sharp, burning pain of the bullet strike him in the right arm, forcing the now-empty Colt from his hand. A third bullet hit Madigan in the lower right side and he slipped from the saddle and hit the ground with a jar.

Madigan must have blacked out for a few seconds. When he came to, the madman was standing over him. O'Neill looked like a rag doll that was shot to pieces. Blood was literally flowing from five gaping holes in his chest, but he stood there with a grin on his face and evil in his eye. And the rifle pointed at Madigan's head was rock steady.

"You lose, Captain!" he sneered as he tightened his finger on the trigger. As Madigan watched a blank look slowly spread across O'Neill's face. O'Neill's body seemed to relax a little and his right leg started to twist under the killer, while the muzzle of the gun swayed off target. O'Neill fought to again bring the barrel in line with Madigan's head but no longer had the strength to do so. His face now took on the appearance of a man that was finally at peace as the once giant of a man slid to the ground, nothing more than a dead pile of flesh. Then Madigan blacked out again.

When he came to again he didn't know how long he had been out. Hours, days, weeks? But somehow he was still alive!

"How?" Madigan groaned when he finally came around again.

"O'Neill died on his feet. Your first two bullets blew his heart away. He was dead and didn't even know it. His evil just kept him going a little longer," Lewana said, as she gently brushed a hair out of Madigan's eye.

THE END

R. Howard Trembly is a pilot, philosopher, professional photographer, and small-business owner in the Pacific Northwest. He has written nonfiction books and several children's stories. MADIGAN is his first published novel.